"I hate you."

"I would expect n[...]
blazed with dark e[...]
to hers.

Kira knew he intended to kiss her, and she knew it wouldn't be gentle. She knew she should push him away—at the very least turn her head. And she knew she would do neither. For she wanted him to kiss her with a desperation that shocked her.

His mouth closed over hers with a hunger that devoured what remained of her will. She shuddered violently and held herself impassive for a heartbeat, knowing capitulation would signal her doom. Then the kiss changed, softened, and a different type of tremor swept through her, stripping her of fear and reason.

She splayed her free hand over his heart, marveling at the strong, rapid beat so in tandem with her own, kissing him in kind. He tasted of exotic spices and seduction, and she suddenly craved both so much she knew she'd die of want if he denied her.

Dear Reader,

My grandmother introduced me to Harlequin
Presents when I was a teenager, and I was
instantly hooked on the exotic settings, deeply
emotional themes and the intense chemistry that
sparked between the spirited heroines and the
compelling alpha heroes.

The popularity of this strong line continues as
Harlequin marks its sixtieth anniversary. I am
honored and thrilled to be part of this celebration
with the debut of my first Harlequin Presents
novel.

I adore swashbuckling pirates, and André Gauthier
embodies that spirit when he captures a woman
caught between loyalty and desire and spirits her
away to his island hideaway. I hope you enjoy
André and Kira's adventure of love as much as I
enjoyed writing it!

Congratulations to Harlequin for sixty years of
riveting love stories! And many thanks to all the
readers, for without you, this milestone wouldn't
be possible.

From my heart to yours,

Janette Kenny
www.jankenny.com

Janette Kenny

PIRATE TYCOON, FORBIDDEN BABY

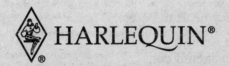

TORONTO • NEW YORK • LONDON
AMSTERDAM • PARIS • SYDNEY • HAMBURG
STOCKHOLM • ATHENS • TOKYO • MILAN • MADRID
PRAGUE • WARSAW • BUDAPEST • AUCKLAND

Recycling programs
for this product may
not exist in your area.

ISBN-13: 978-0-373-12840-2

PIRATE TYCOON, FORBIDDEN BABY

First North American Publication 2009.

All about the author...
Janette Kenny

For as long as **JANETTE KENNY** can remember, plots and characters have taken up residence in her head. Her parents, both voracious readers, read her the classics when she was a child. That gave birth to a deep love for literature, and allowed her to travel to exotic locales—those found between the covers of books.

Janette's artist mother encouraged her yen to write. As an adolescent she began creating cartoons featuring her dad as the hero, with plots that focused on the misadventures on their family farm, and she stuffed them in the nightly newspaper for him to find. To her frustration, her sketches paled in comparison to her captions.

Her first real writing began with fan fiction, taking favorite TV shows and writing the episodes and endings she loved—happily ever after, of course. In her junior year of high school she told her literature teacher she intended to write for a living one day. His advice? Pursue the dream, but don't quit the day job.

Though she dabbled with articles, she didn't fully embrace her dream to write novels until years later, when she was a busy cosmetologist making a name for herself in her own salon. That was when she decided to write the type of stories she'd been reading—romances.

Once the writing bug bit, the incurable passion for creating stories and peopling them consumed her. Still, it was seven more years and that many novels before she saw her first historical romance published. Now that she's also writing contemporary romances for Harlequin, she finally knows that a full-time career in writing is closer to reality.

Janette shares her home and free time with a chow-shepherd pup she rescued from the pound, who aspires to be a lapdog. She invites you to visit her Web site at www.jankenny.com. She loves to hear from readers—e-mail her at janette@jankenny.com.

CHAPTER ONE

KIRA MONTGOMERY pressed her forehead against the massage table's padded face cradle and shifted again to loosen the tension knotting her shoulders and neck. Impossible.

Her masseuse had "stepped out for a moment." The term obviously meant something different to her than it did to Kira. Leaving a client waiting fifteen minutes was unsuitable.

Chateau Mystique couldn't afford more bad press. The tragic deaths and ensuing scandals associated with the five-star hotel on the Las Vegas strip had hurt business. Hurt her in ways she'd never imagined.

To make her life more of a jumble, her doctor had confirmed the one thing she'd never anticipated. She was pregnant.

Her insides quivered and she took a deep breath. Held it. Let it out slowly. It didn't help. Nothing helped.

Ever since she'd heeded her solicitor's advice and traveled to the Caribbean island of Petit St. Marc for a closed meeting with André Gauthier, her life had tumbled into a chaotic nightmare. The devastatingly handsome billionaire had denied ever knowing of their meeting, and had refused to divulge how he'd gained stock in her hotel. Though she'd been frustrated and angry, she'd been captivated by the sheer power of his persona and his rapier-quick ability to debate an issue.

He'd mentally stimulated her and physically aroused her more than any man she'd ever met. But she wouldn't be swayed by his staggering offer to buy out her shares. He owned minority stock, and that was all he'd ever have.

The Chateau was her home. Her dream. Her legacy. There'd been no reason to tarry on the island any longer.

No reason except desire. She hadn't been able to deny the passion blazing between them and the raw hunger he stirred in her. And why should she?

She was an adult. Surely she could engage in a brief affair and walk away?

But thirteen weeks later she hadn't been able to forget their stolen night of passion. Or the scandal that had erupted the following morning to rip them apart. Or André Gauthier, the father of her child, the man who'd recently made headlines with his ruthless attempt to break Bellamy Enterprises.

Would the shareholders force Peter Bellamy to sell his father's empire? Would they decide to defy André and set the stage for a hostile takeover?

Perhaps they'd agree to a merger. Yes, a nice peaceful working arrangement, like the one she'd thought to forge with André before she learned of his perfidy.

How naïve she'd been. Where she'd only worried about dealing with André over the Chateau, she now fretted over the merger of them as parents. How did one tell a chance lover that he'd soon be a father—a chance lover she'd parted with on hostile terms?

The nausea that had been her constant companion the past few weeks threatened to return. She concentrated on the doctor's instructions instead of dwelling on ringing up André again to relay her news.

One dragon at a time. That was the only way she'd come out of this debacle intact. She'd left a message for him to contact her. And if he didn't. If he chose to ignore her…

The door opened behind Kira, and she quickly pushed her worries about André to the back of her mind to confront the tardy masseuse. "I trust you have a good excuse for leaving me here waiting for so long?"

Silence answered her.

Kira frowned at the floor, willing away the dark premonition that crept into the room like a cold London fog roiling off the Thames. But her trepidation only grew, because she knew someone stood in the doorway, watching her.

Someone, she sensed, who shouldn't be here.

She stilled, her breath catching in her throat as a wedge of light arrowed across the plush carpet and darted beneath the table to inch up the wall.

A chill born of anxiety hopscotched up her spine, and she shivered despite the luxurious blanket draped over her bare body. "Who's there?"

"Bonjour, ma chérie," he said, his deep, rough-edged voice causing her heart to race so fast her head spun.

André Gauthier! Instead of returning her call, he'd come to her. Her first impulse was to scramble off the table and launch herself into his arms, just to assure herself this wasn't a dream. Just to touch him, kiss him.

"I suggest we wait to talk until later, when I'm presentable," she said, in an effort to gain control of her rioting emotions.

"I didn't come here to chat."

A pair of obscenely expensive men's loafers stepped into the view afforded her through the face cradle, the hem of his charcoal trousers breaking perfectly on his vamps.

He splayed a hand on the small of her back, the heat of his palm sensuously electric, branding her, reminding her that the last time he'd touched her thusly she'd been awash with passion. Not that she needed a reminder.

But where she'd sensed his ardor before, she perceived his antagonism now. All directed at her.

His anger didn't bode well for what she must tell him.

"Then why are you here?" The tremor in her voice conveyed her trepidation and confusion.

"To claim what is mine."

She dug her fingernails into the armrest, likely scoring the butter-soft leather. Of course. He was here to haggle with her over the Chateau again.

Kira had expected this quarrel. Yet in her imaginings she'd been dressed and in control of her emotions, at the board meeting scheduled two weeks from now, not naked and quivering with apprehension and need. Surely she didn't wish to feel sexually receptive to him? But his presence commanded all her senses.

He glided a hand up her spine, sliding the blanket over her sensitized skin slowly, and the desire churning to life within her silenced the protests in her head. She gritted her teeth, fighting the feelings erupting in her: annoyance, desire, need.

It was a losing battle.

From the very first time they'd met she'd been in tune to his every breath, to the way he filled a room with his intensity. To the way his unique scent of spice tempered with the tang of the sea called to her, stripping her inhibitions bare.

His long fingers danced over her bared back in a silken caress, flooding her with unbidden memories of the intoxicating kisses that she'd craved, of masterful hands that had brought her to the pinnacle of pleasure and beyond, and lovemaking that had been more intense, more consuming than anything she'd experienced in her life.

That firm, yet gentle caress muddled her thinking. Her body reacted to him with shocking welcome, her breasts growing heavy, the sensitive nipples peaking.

She bit back a sigh of pleasure, her emotions roiling in utter turmoil. A heavy ache of want converged at the apex of her thighs, spreading upward, making her quake with desire. Damn him!

One caress had reduced her to a quivering wanton, sweeping her away on a wave of raw need. She detested his power over her. Hated the magnetism that drew her to the powerful throb of his touch.

Kira forced her voice to remain steady when her emotions were anything but. "This isn't the place to discuss business."

"I disagree."

The crackle of paper echoed in the tense stillness. A pristine white sheet was thrust beneath the face cradle.

She huffed out an annoyed breath, expecting another decadently outlandish offer for the Chateau. Her gaze skimmed the header, and her stomach plummeted as her world tipped on its axis.

No! This couldn't be! She read each damning word, her racing heart nearly stopping as the meaning sank into her soul. How could she have believed her future was safe from his power, from his dominance?

"What trickery is this?" she asked.

"No tricks, *ma chérie*. I own majority shares in Chateau Mystique."

Impossible! Edouard's shares were to pass into her hands after his will was read in two weeks. He'd promised she'd have majority control of the hotel then.

Yet the document proved Edouard's shares had fallen into this arrogant billionaire's hands. She doubted its validity, even though her solicitor's signature was there, a signature she'd seen countless times. This couldn't have happened, yet it had.

She felt betrayed. Used. Abandoned all over again.

André controlled her hotel. Her home. And he'd control her if she let him.

His hand glided over her shoulders in a mock caress, the fingers playing her skin like a fine instrument. Only the dirge sang her doom. She trembled, her mind reeling, more furious than she'd ever been in her life.

He laughed, no doubt gloating over his conquest and her reaction to him, and her humiliation was absolute. "Get up."

Kira sprang up so fast the room spun. She clasped the blanket around her heaving chest and shook her head to toss her heavy hair away from her face, too gripped with shock and anger to feel satisfaction when his eyes flared with sensual awareness, with masculine appreciation.

At least they were alone. She'd read that whenever André

left his island compound his trusted guard accompanied him. The brute was undoubtedly in the hall, making sure nobody interrupted his decadently wealthy employer.

Her gaze climbed André's tall, muscular form, clad in an impeccably tailored charcoal suit that shimmered in the artificial light. French, of course, the cut emphasizing his long powerful legs, lean hips and broad shoulders.

His snow-white shirt was a startling contrast against his darkly tanned skin, and his silvery tie complemented his platinum watchband that had probably cost more than what she earned in a year. His thick black hair was combed off his brow, his clothing meticulous, his bearing indomitable.

Her heart did a traitorous flutter as she remembered how much she'd savored having his powerful body molded to hers, those elegant hands bringing her to pleasure again and again. Drowning in the passion in his eyes as they'd made love.

It had been this way from the start. Less than two hours after she'd met him they'd had sex: hot, wild, urgent. There had been no love involved, only an overpowering attraction and an intense demanding need.

She'd never behaved so recklessly in her life. Never thought of the consequences of falling into André's bed.

Tell him the result of the affair, her mind screamed. Get it out in the open now.

Hands trembling, she dug her cold fingers into the blanket and met his eyes, such an intense dark brown they gleamed black. A dizzying rush of emotions slammed into her, staggering her with their strength. No, now wasn't the time.

"Get dressed," he said.

Kira turned her back to him and slipped a blue silk sundress over her flushed body, hating the way her hands shook and how her body pulsed and quivered with awareness of him. Though the garment she donned was modest, she felt exposed under his knowing stare. Vulnerable.

"I assume you expect to buy my shares now?" she said.

"*Oui.*"

"They aren't for sale."

"You haven't heard my offer."

"I don't need to." She faced him, head high, her insides tangled in a riot of emotions. My God, he was an extraordinarily gorgeous man—tall, bronzed, strong, like a god come to life. And he was just as arrogant, just as domineering.

"I'm not selling," she said.

One dark eyebrow lifted, as if challenging her statement. "Everyone has a price."

"I don't."

"We shall see." André nodded to the door. "After you."

"I'll say my goodbye to you here, and see you at the board meeting in two weeks."

His smile was glacial. "You're coming with me, *ma chérie.*"

Her skin pebbled as a cloying sensation settled over her. "In your dreams," she said, hating the tremor in her voice.

A muscle pulsed madly in his cheek. "I'll carry you if I must, but we are returning to Petit St. Marc."

The island? Her heart stuttered, then began racing. "Why?"

"To trump your lover, *ma chérie.*"

Had he gone mad? "Then you are wasting your time, because I don't have a lover."

"I know you've been doing Peter Bellamy's bidding from the start. Now it stops."

"Peter?" A hysterical laugh bubbled from her. "I assure you that I'm not his lover."

"Spare me your lies. I know the truth."

No, he couldn't be more wrong. But she realized that if he didn't believe her in this, he'd never believe he was the father of her child.

"I'm not going anywhere with you. Leave now or I'll—"

He snapped his fingers and she jumped, slamming her back against the wall. "That's all it would take to have this hotel razed. Your shares would be worthless. Is that what you want?"

This was blackmail. Kidnapping at the very least! But to balk would bring about the destruction of her hotel.

"No," she said, knowing he wasn't bluffing. "But I can't leave the Chateau without making arrangements."

"You can and you will." His long fingers curled around her bare arm and he guided her out the door, his touch surprisingly gentle.

Yet she felt the underlying steel and rage in him and knew fighting was futile. And she was so weary already.

André was a man who took what he wanted, when he wanted. He'd proved that when he'd seduced her on Petit St. Marc. Proved it again when he'd swum in from the Caribbean like a great white shark and gobbled up control of the Chateau.

Yet she'd glimpsed another side of him on the island—a tenderness that had called to her heart, and a vulnerability she hadn't understood.

Yes, for now she'd return to the island with him. Perhaps there she'd find the right time to tell him about their child. Perhaps there she'd be able to reason with him about the Chateau—convince him she'd been robbed of her birthright. Perhaps in time they'd be able to start over.

André Gauthier stared at the deceptive woman walking down the corridor before him, her rounded hips rocking in an invitation that any red-blooded man would accept. No wonder Bellamy had given her forty-nine percent of Chateau Mystique.

Kira Montgomery was sex personified. She had certainly beguiled *him* with the oldest trick in the book.

He'd prided himself on his cool control under duress, nurtured it until it was second nature. It had never let him down—until Kira had invaded his island three months ago.

André hadn't been surprised when Bellamy had sent a female employee to Petit St. Marc to charm him after his last offer to buy the Chateau had been turned down. The excuse that she'd come for a prearranged meeting had been a lie.

The old man had banked on Kira's charms and André's

moment of grief to alter his ultimate goal. Or so André had believed.

It had worked. For that one night. Kira had pleaded her case with passion, and André had found himself caught up in the most stimulating debate of his life.

He hadn't realized the extend of her deceit until much later. The elder Bellamy hadn't sent her—his son had. Peter. His most fierce rival. Peter—the man he now suspected had set in motion events that had brought about the accident that had killed Edouard's mistress and landed Edouard in a hospital.

Kira was not only Peter's mistress, she was his accomplice as well. *Oui*, she was the brains of the maneuver that had ultimately eliminated the old man—that had earned her control of Chateau Mystique.

But her treachery had robbed André of something far more valuable than property. She'd had a hand in destroying the last of his family.

Kira had deceived him in the worst possible way.

She deserved no less in return.

Retribution coursed through his blood like a molten river.

Peter Bellamy would chaff, knowing that André held Kira on Petit St. Marc. She in turn wouldn't be able to contact her accomplice—her lover.

She'd be at his mercy when he launched the final takeover of Bellamy Enterprises.

His revenge wouldn't be satisfied until he'd bested Bellamy's conniving son at his own game—until he'd made Kira regret that she'd set out to destroy him.

André joined her in the lift and they rode up in silence to the fifth floor. He wondered if she'd entertained Peter Bellamy there while the old man had dominated his mistress in the penthouse.

The dark thought stayed with him as he followed Kira to a fifth-floor door. She slid a card key in the slot and stepped into a small but cozy suite. He noted the room bore quaint personal touches, typical of an English parlor, and carried her light floral fragrance. It seemed too benign. Too cozy.

"Pack light," he said, annoyed by the thought of her entertaining Peter Bellamy here.

Her shoulders stiffened—proof the order had grated. Good. He wanted to keep her off balance, keep her wondering what he planned to do to her.

"Do you plan to keep me locked in a room?" she asked.

"If I must."

The color leached from her face, only to return in a rosy flush that hinted of righteous anger. He ground his teeth, annoyed she could project such a quality.

"This is wrong of you to force me to leave here," she said.

How dared she accuse *him* of wrongdoing? "You should have thought of that before you agreed to do Bellamy's bidding."

She stared at him, her expression guarded. "As I've said all along, I was told you'd agreed to meet me on your island to discuss the Chateau."

"Save your lies," he said. "I have proof of your part in his scheme."

Her lovely mouth fell open, as if she was shocked by his claim. "I have absolutely no idea what you're referring to."

His smile was as tight as the tension bouncing off the jade brocade walls. "It amazes me that people shred the paper trail but forget the electronic one."

"There is none," she said.

"Don't be too sure."

"But I am certain."

"Then you're a fool."

She flushed, but instead of continuing her defense she looked away from him. Guilt? It must be.

André smiled. He'd caught her. Her game was over, and his was just beginning.

"Enough wasting time," he said, eager to leave this place that pulsed with bad memories.

She moved into her bedroom like someone walking to the guillotine. Soundlessly she rolled a case from the closet. The damned thing was half as tall as she.

When he realized her intent, he took it from her and hefted it onto the bed. "Take only the essentials."

"I'll pack what I wish to," she said, her amber eyes too bright with moisture.

Her tears had no effect on him. He'd learned long ago from his mother and sister that women cried over everything and nothing just to get their way. He certainly wouldn't allow Bellamy's mistress to beguile him again.

His mobile phone chirped and he immediately answered it. The tone signaled it came from his guard. "What?"

"Peter Bellamy just arrived."

André cut a sharp glance to Kira, who seemed preoccupied packing her bag. She'd not been out of his sight, so either Bellamy was making a surprise visit to the Chateau to see his lover, or someone on Kira's staff had phoned him.

"Watch him." André slipped his mobile in his pocket. "How much longer are you going to dawdle over what to take?"

"I only need a few more things, and my files." She moved to a desk and secured a laptop. "Everything is here so I can keep abreast of the hotel."

"You cannot mean to continue working?"

"I'm not one to sit around and while away my time." She flicked him a defiant glare and slipped the laptop in a carryon. "And I don't require your permission."

"Do not be too sure of that."

André had the satisfaction of watching her face drain of color before his mobile chirped again. He answered it curtly.

"Paparazzi just arrived," his guard said. "They're swarming around Peter Bellamy."

Damn. The last thing André wanted to do was engage in another public confrontation with Kira and the media at the start of his takeover.

He met her questioning gaze. "We need to leave without the gossipmongers seeing us. Unless you prefer a repeat of our last encounter?"

She flushed crimson and shook her head. He feared she'd balk—that she'd court the media's attention again. "The service entrance is our best choice."

He repeated that to his guard. "Meet us in five minutes."

"But I'm not ready yet," she said.

He swore and checked his watch. "You have three minutes. Then we leave, no matter your state of dress." He gaze slid over her body, openly appreciating her curves. "Or undress."

She stiffened, as if ready to argue.

He fed on his annoyance and tapped a finger on his watch. "You're down to two minutes and forty-five seconds."

Mumbling an oath, she grabbed lacy undergarments from a drawer and ran to the walk-in closet. He made to follow.

"Don't you dare come closer," she said, making him wonder if she could read minds.

"I wouldn't dream of it." He strode to her suitcase, zipped it shut and heaved it from the bed.

With five seconds to spare, she stepped from the dressing room wearing a floral skirt that hugged her firm bottom and thighs and stopped above her knees to accentuate the curve of her calves and dainty ankles. A fashionable summer sweater in a clear turquoise molded the full bosom he knew filled his hands. She stepped into sling heels that were sexy as hell, and tossed a smaller bag into her carryon.

She zipped it shut with impatient finality. Her small hand closed around the reinforced handles, her intent clear.

"I'll take that." André slung the strap over his shoulder.

She grabbed her purse and slipped a mobile inside it. He took the bag from her and removed the phone, setting it high on a shelf. "So you managed to ring Peter after all?"

"I left a message for my solicitor."

"I trust you bade him *au revoir*, for we leave now, Kira."
André held the door for her.

She glanced once at the shelf, then swept past him, her head
high. He smiled and followed. She moved with a staccato
click of heels and a beguiling sway of her hips down the
corridor to the lifts.

Oui, enjoying her luscious body would assuage his rage.

She stepped inside the lift and he joined her, wrestling the
baggage behind them and forcing her closer to him.

The doors started to shut. The ones on the car directly across
from theirs opened in perfect synchronization.

In that split second, when each had a full view of the
opposite lift, André locked gazes with Peter Bellamy. His rival
fixed a black scowl on him, then looked sharply to André's side,
where Kira stood.

Bellamy stared, then his mouth dropped open as he realized
his lover, his deceitful accomplice, was at his enemy's side. His
furious gaze snapped back to André.

André smiled, draped an arm around Kira's slender shoulder,
and gave his arch rival a smart salute.

CHAPTER TWO

KIRA wondered if this day would ever end as she exchanged André's private jet for the limousine waiting for them at Aimé Césaire International Airport. And what had her solicitor made of the harried message she'd left him?

She had no way of knowing. At least the flight from Las Vegas to Martinique had gone smoothly, but nearly fourteen hours of travel had exhausted her.

André's stony silence had drained the last of her energy. She'd hoped to talk with him rationally on the flight, but he'd closed himself off from her. Now she was in no mood to engage in heartfelt conversation with him.

Her summer-weight sweater smothered her, and the skirt she'd thought would be refined and comfortable hung like a limp rag. The island humidity, vastly different from the dry Nevada air, urged her heavy hair into the natural curl that she'd struggled to straighten all of her life. She was sure the make-up she'd applied before André dragged her from the Chateau was gone.

But she had the satisfaction of not being the only one wearied by the trip. Though André's perfectly tailored suit retained the crisp lines that complemented the brooding intensity of his dark eyes and matched his arrogance, dark stubble delineated his arrogantly handsome face.

That rogue's shadow emphasized the grim set of his mouth and gave him a dangerously sexy look. She caught herself remembering how those firm lips had felt moving against hers, tearing down her defenses and arresting her fears. How his hands and mouth and powerful body had brought her to her first shattering climax, and then continued to do so more times than she could recall, until she'd been deliciously sated and more happy than she'd ever been.

That had been the calm before the storm. What she couldn't fathom was what tempest now brewed in André, as the limo raced past fields of sugar cane toward Fort-de-France.

Three months ago, on his island, they'd both expressed that they never wished to see the other again in the heat of anger. Yet she'd rung him, and he'd come for her. Or had he planned to come to the Chateau anyway, to steal her away?

She suspected that was the case, as he hadn't even asked why she'd contacted him. And with his anger heating the very air she breathed, it was better she hold her secret a bit longer.

Too weary to make sense of this nightmare, she stretched her legs to ease the dull ache in her back. Like the other drivers racing down the boulevard in a hurry to get to their homes, she was anxious to get settled for the day.

This extended close proximity to André wreaked havoc on her senses. Every subtle shift of his powerful body, every heated glance, each casual touch, muddled her mind more and more.

A dozen times she'd nearly blurted out that she was pregnant with his child. Let him deal with *that*! But his brooding silence had stopped her.

He barely resembled the teasing rogue she'd met on Petit St. Marc. The man who'd baited and lured her into rousing debate, who'd flirted shamelessly with her. Who'd made love to her with unbridled passion and made her feel wanted, if only for a moment.

He'd withdrawn from her like a wounded animal. She debated scooting closer and taking him into her arms. Intuition told her he wouldn't welcome her gesture of comfort and empathy.

Kira bit her lower lip, exhausted and pensive. She'd never been this undone by a man, and her lack of control over her emotions mortified her. But then, she'd never been plunked into the middle of a dark drama without a script either.

She shifted on her seat as traffic slowed and the sleek white limo crawled past La Savane. Palms towered over the public gardens, lush with greenery and a profusion of flowers. How sad she'd not had time to visit the gardens when she was here before. She certainly wouldn't ask André for a tour now.

As they neared the harbor, quaint shops and houses were stacked against the hills like colorful children's blocks in bright crayon colors. A reggae beat from the market area danced in the air, yet the silence in the limo throbbed to the weary cadence of her heart.

"How much longer?" she asked, glancing at the harbor, where the docked sailboats resembled a denuded forest.

André gave a terse shrug, drawing her attention from the impressive breadth of his shoulders to the fatigue lines etched under his eyes. His was an intense gaze that seemed to look right through her. "An hour and a half at the most."

No rest or respite anytime soon, then. She took small consolation in the fact he looked as weary as she felt.

Not for the first time she suspected he'd left near midnight to arrive in Las Vegas early this morning. Perhaps, like she, he'd had a sleepless night.

But where he'd likely dwelled on blackmailing her to leave the Chateau, her mind had spun with the miracle of motherhood. For the first time in her life she'd no longer be alone.

Kira rested a hand on her stomach and smiled. Last night she hadn't been concerned about the hours ticking by while she lay in bed in wonder, awed by the precious baby growing in her.

She'd tried to envision how her life was about to change—had debated how she should let André know. She'd naïvely believed impending fatherhood might mellow him, that what they'd shared once could grow into something meaningful.

Love? Yes, the possibility of that blooming between them

had played over in her mind as well, teasing her with how good her future with him could be.

For the first time in ages she'd taken a peek at the school-girl imaginings she'd painted in the dark of night back in the days of her youth, when she'd dreamed her prince would ride in on a white horse and whisk her away to his castle, where they'd live happily ever after. When she'd fall in love forever, and not just for a stolen moment.

Not once had she thought André would sail back into her life this morning like a bloodthirsty pirate, with pillaging and revenge burning in his soul. That he'd accuse her of joining forces with Peter to ruin him. If he only knew the truth.

No, if only he'd *believe* the truth!

She shut her eyes against cold, hard reality. Instead of a white horse bearing her to a castle, a white limo raced her toward an uncertain future. Instead of her prince gazing at her with loving eyes, André barely spared her a glance.

What would he do when she told him she carried his child? Accept his responsibility with resigned indifference, as her father had done? Surely he wasn't that cold, that callous?

"What's wrong?" André asked, his warm breath fanning her face. "Are you ill?"

I'm pregnant. She looked up at him, prepared to tell him, but his eyes were as dark and turbulent as a winter storm. She was simply too weary to brave the gale now.

"I was just—" Caught in a fairytale. But they never come true. Never. "I'm just tired. It's been a long journey."

He stared at her for a tense moment, his expression shifting to the hard, indifferent mask she'd come to hate. "You can rest on the boat."

Kira laughed to herself as he moved to his side of the limo again, though the space between them afforded her no comfort. The express ferry she'd taken to and from the island before had provided seating, but no place where she could put her feet up.

Right now her ankles felt hot and swollen. Strange, since

she'd refrained from satisfying her thirst so she wouldn't spend the whole flight in the tiny restroom.

She stared at the glistening expanse of Flamands Bay, where a cruise ship dwarfed the catamarans and yachts that bobbed lazily in a turquoise sea. A welcoming breeze sent the palm fronds swaying, and gentled the tide to a mesmerizing ripple touched with gold. But she feared she couldn't tolerate much more travel without succumbing to motion sickness.

That certainly wasn't the way she wished to alert André of her condition. In fact, she was totally lost on how to broach the subject in light of today's shocking events and his aggressive mood.

André exited the limo the second it stopped, as if anxious to get away from her. Fine. She welcomed the reprieve. But it was short-lived again. Instead of the driver helping her out, the handsome billionaire, unyielding and resolute, opened her door.

He extended an exquisitely manicured hand to her. She stared at it, at the fingers long and graceful, the tanned skin smooth and dusted with black hair.

Memories of those hands skimming over her naked flesh and bringing her to pleasure time and again tormented her. There was nothing of her body he hadn't touched. Including her heart?

"I won't bite," he said, the arrogant tilt to his mouth hinting the opposite.

Not that she needed to be reminded. "You did before."

She saw her own burning need flickering in his eyes and gasped. A flush stole over her, and she chided herself for reminding him of their night together.

"I wasn't the only one with teeth, *ma chérie*." He took her hand, and the electricity that zinged from him staggered her.

Kira wanted to jerk away, but couldn't. She wanted to lean into him, but didn't dare.

The warmth of his skin and his steely power made her feel safe when she was anything but. How pathetic she must be.

Only a fool would fantasize about the man who'd accused her of bringing the paparazzi to his island. Who'd somehow acquired majority shares in her hotel. Who'd forced her to return to his island, where she'd experienced blazing passion. Where they'd created a child.

Kira forced her feet to move, grateful the setting sun had taken the heat out of the day. Yet a more dangerous warmth replaced it as she kept pace with André toward the waterfront, his hand firmly grasping hers, his narrowed gaze seeming to look beyond the people around them.

A few native workers near the boatyard glanced their way as they passed, speaking in a rich patois accented with French. She could only make out a word or two—greetings, mostly, interspersed with his name. Obviously the billionaire was known here, but no one attempted to engage him in talk.

Several express taxis were moored at the ferry terminal, their gangplanks crowded with a blend of tourists, transplanted islanders and native Caribs. The thought of joining that mass of humanity made her break her out in a nervous sweat.

At the dock, André guided her away from the larger craft. All she saw were small speedboats, bobbing wildly in the water. Her stomach lifted, then slammed down again as she scanned the jetty for a larger vessel.

None were moored along its length. None!

"Please tell me you don't expect me to ride in one of those little boats?" she asked.

"*Oui*, a dinghy. It is the fastest way."

She held back—not easy, considering his strength and the way her knees knocked. "No, I can't."

He stared down at her, his lean features resolute, his dark eyes intense. "You've no choice."

She swallowed her panic and closed her eyes, struggling to calm the riotous beat of her heart. "Small boats terrify me."

"You've nothing to fear."

Was he joking? No, the taut line of his jaw shadowed with stubble told her he was dead serious.

Panic clawed at her throat. As a child, she'd nearly died in a boating accident on Lake Mead. That memory and its devastating aftermath still haunted her.

She wouldn't, couldn't, get in a small boat.

Kira jerked free, but before she could bolt up the pier he swept her into his arms. She squirmed, then went still as death as he stepped down into the rocking boat.

She flung her arms around his neck and clung like a sandbur, her heart beating so hard she knew he must feel it too. Each gasp for air drew the spicy scent of him deeper into her lungs, further muddling her senses.

A laugh rumbled from him, at odds with the ferocious temperament he'd shown thus far. "Relax, *ma chérie*. See that cruiser anchored in the bay?"

She reluctantly lifted her face from the shelter of his warm neck. A sleek white cabin cruiser gleamed like a pearl against the caramel-tinged sunset. But it was so far away.

"You'll be perfectly safe on the *Sans Doute*."

Her mouth formed a soundless "oh."

André set her on her feet, his own braced wide as the boat rose and fell with the tide. He rattled off instructions in French to the boy manning the motor.

The engine powered up. André sat on the bench and pulled her down beside him. Her stomach pitched and her skin turned clammy, despite the refreshing seaspray.

She trembled with bone-deep fear. Her hand gripped the single handhold so tightly her fingers went numb.

He stared at her, his brows slammed together. "*Mon Dieu*, you *are* afraid."

She gave a jerky nod.

He wrapped an arm around her shoulders, one hand making soothing circles on her arm. "Relax."

If only she could. The dinghy raced away, the hull rising as they picked up speed. Her insides quivered and snapped like the nautical flags on nearby boats. She buried her face against his chest, her mind trapped in a nightmare.

"Look at me. *Mon Dieu*, look at me!"

She met his penetrating gaze, knowing hers was wide with fright, but uncaring what he thought of her. "I hate you."

"I would expect no less from you." His eyes blazed with dark emotion as his head lowered to hers.

Kira knew he intended to kiss her, and she knew it wouldn't be gentle. She knew she should push him away— at the very least turn her head. And she knew she would do neither. For she wanted him to kiss her with a desperation that shocked her.

His mouth closed over hers with a hunger that devoured what remained of her will. She shuddered violently and held herself impassive for a heartbeat, knowing capitulation would signal her doom. Then the kiss changed, softened, and a different type of tremor swept through her, stripping her of reason.

She splayed her free hand over his heart, marveling at the strong rapid beat so in tandem with her own, kissing him in kind. He tasted of exotic spices and seduction, and she suddenly craved both so much she knew she'd die of want if he denied her.

As the boat cut across the waves, the rhythmic duel of their tongues and the ravenous glide of lips on skin consumed her with memories. She was lost. Adrift at sea with her corporate pirate. Enslaved to the sensations she'd only known with him.

His long strong fingers played an erotic melody on her back that made her heart sing and her body hum with need. Like a rosebud caressed by the sun, she blossomed in his arms, kissing him back with all the hunger she'd denied for so long.

He'd done nothing to earn her trust, yet she felt safe in his arms. Wanted. So she simply gave up rational thought and relished this moment.

Too soon he pulled away, when she would've begged him to touch her breasts, her sex.

"We've reached the *Sans Doute*, *ma chérie*, and you are safe."

It was a lie. As long as she surrendered to his slightest touch she was in mortal danger of losing her heart and soul to this enigmatic man.

André prided himself on his rigid control in the boardroom and the bedroom, yet kissing Kira had been a mistake. He'd done it to take her mind off her crippling fear. But he'd come close to losing control of the situation.

She wasn't an innocent, yet he'd felt hesitation ripple through her, felt her lips tremble against his, felt her fear of the sea. Then that whispered moan of surrender had sung through his blood and instinct had taken over.

She was an enchantress. A sea witch. Now she was his.

He helped her climb onto the aft deck of the *Sans Doute*, mindful of her shaky posture and her frantic hold on his hand, the nails digging in so deep they'd leave a mark. He was gripped with the sudden urge to hold her, protect her, make love to her until her fears dissipated.

Mon Dieu, he hated this raging desire that threatened to burn out of control for her. Hated the role she'd played in Bellamy's life. Hated that he admired her pluck, that she hadn't resorted to tears, threats or seduction once.

He escorted Kira up the circular stairs and propelled her through the main salon, dressed in the richest golden sateen and deepest burgundy velour, then up to the observation salon. His hand rested at the beguiling curve of her back—in part because he enjoyed touching her, and also because he knew it bothered her. He wanted her hot and bothered.

The bullet lights in the ceiling shot platinum and bronze streaks through her wealth of mahogany hair that his fingers itched to sift through. But she would not welcome his touch now. She was as flighty as a hummingbird, the pulse-point in her throat warbling to a frantic beat.

Still he ached to draw her close, to press his mouth over that spot, feel the beat of her heart match time with his. She'd not fight him. No, she'd melt in his arms—if only to take her mind off her fear.

That was reason enough to bide his time. It was imperative she crave his touch. That he earn her trust.

It shouldn't be difficult to do, considering she'd been groomed to pleasure a man. *Oui*, before he was through she'd beg him to bed her.

It was inevitable—a fact Bellamy must be aware of. So why hadn't his enemy contacted him yet?

"Make yourself comfortable." He strode across the lounge to the bar. "Would you care for a drink before we get underway?"

"Water, please."

He slipped behind the granite-topped bar and slid her a look. She'd taken a seat on the circular sofa, her legs curled beneath her and an overstuffed pillow hugged to her stomach. Her complexion was paler than before.

A spark of alarm hit him again. "Are you all right?"

"I'm just thirsty." She flicked him an uncertain glance. "It's been too long since I drank any water." She shook her head as if dismissing the matter.

Another ploy to gather sympathy? To heap guilt on him for dragging her to the island against her will?

Of course. She'd only had to ask at any time and he would have made sure she was refreshed, that she was comfortable. He wasn't an ogre, determined to make her suffer physically.

He poured sparkling water into a glass, added a twist of lime and took it to her. Annoyance burned his soul as he handed her the glass.

She took it, a telling gasp escaping her as their fingers brushed. "Thank you."

"My pleasure," André said, which was far from the truth.

He stalked back to the bar and prepared a simple rum daiquiri with the barest squeeze of lime. Thoughts of Kira making love with Bellamy sped through his mind and left a white froth of rage in its wake.

Instead of savoring the heavy, rich swirl of rum, André tasted bitter revenge coating his tongue. Spending half a day with her had sharpened his senses to a razor's edge.

Kira portrayed the *ingénue* when she was anything but innocent. *Oui*, he knew her for what she truly was, for he'd tasted her passion. One sip demanded more.

Every nuance of her was branded on his mind. The occasional tremor that rocked her, leaving her shaken. The pensive look he glimpsed in her eyes when she thought nobody was watching. Those odd moments when she rested a hand on her stomach and the most beauteous expression came over her.

It was as if she was sharing a secret with someone.

Well, he had secrets of his own. Dark, disturbing ones that robbed him of sleep.

"Do you have reliable internet on the island?" she asked.

"*Oui*. I have a private satellite connection in my office." *She* would have limited access, at his discretion, and monitored. He prowled the carpeted salon and sipped his drink, her question spiking his suspicion. "Thinking of begging Peter to rescue you from the situation you've both created? Or do you need his instructions on how best to spy on me?"

Color streaked across her high cheekbones and her amber eyes snapped, her anger and defiance charging the air. "I intend to run my hotel from my prison."

"You mean *my* hotel."

"You are the majority stockholder now, but the Chateau will always be mine."

His fingers tightened on his glass. She couldn't be more wrong, but he'd let her hold her confidence for now. He took no pleasure in beating someone who was so near the edge.

The dark smudges beneath her eyes attested that she was close to exhaustion. Yet her narrow shoulders remained squared and her chin high, as if she was refusing to accept that she stood on thin ice regarding the Chateau—regarding him.

Her quiet strength intrigued him. He'd expected her to use

her delectable body to court his favor, to deceive him more. But though she'd responded instantly to his touch, his kiss, she hadn't attempted to take the initiative with him. Yet.

He tossed back his daiquiri as his anger burned anew. What was her game?

It didn't matter. He'd have his revenge in the end. He had proof Peter had sent her to Petit St. Marc to seduce him, *and* alerted the paparazzi, and he now held documents proving her part in the deadly plot she and Peter had instigated.

The latter was enough to make him despise her. He hated that she'd acquired the Chateau with her deceit. Hated that she was Bellamy's mistress. Hated that her solemn amber eyes had the power to make him question his plans.

He set his glass on the bar with a thunk and strode to her, his annoyance sparking like lightning when she lifted her chin and stared up at him, wide-eyed but unflinching. She was driving him mad, for he'd never wanted to intimidate a woman until now.

In one fluid movement he rested a knee on the cushions before her curled legs, braced one hand on the sofa's arm and the other on its back. "I own Chateau Mystique and I own you. Never doubt you are both in my control."

Her full lips thinned. "That is barbarous."

"Perhaps you were unaware the blood of pirates courses through my veins?" He yanked away the pillow shielding her and splayed his fingers on her stomach, his thumb resting on her *mons* and his fingers grazing the swell of her breasts.

She gasped, eyes huge and dark, with awakening desire. The pulse in the ivory column of her neck throbbed to a savage tempo that mirrored his own erratic heartbeat.

Oui. She didn't fear him. She wanted him as much as he wanted her. In this they were equal. But not for long.

André affected a rapacious grin. "What? You have nothing to say?"

A tremor vibrated through her into him as she shoved his

hand from her, but her eyes were still smoky with passion. "Nothing that you'd believe."

"Save your professions of innocence." He lurched from her and stared at her expressive eyes that challenged him. "Relax, *ma chérie*. I have no intention of ravishing you. At least not yet."

She looked away, satisfying him that she understood his dismissal as well as his promise. The inevitability.

"Not ever," she said, the words whispered, yet fierce.

The challenge hung between them—a cold, invisible wall that he longed to tear down.

André stalked across the salon and bounded up the stairs to the sundeck, knowing he was a hair's breadth from toppling Kira back on the sumptuous sofa and showing her just how much she hungered for his touch. How easily she'd capitulate.

Now wasn't the time. They were spent from the journey. In thirty minutes they'd land at Petit St. Marc. That wasn't nearly enough time to enjoy her charms, and he fully intended to savor every inch of Kira at his leisure, for bedding her would enrage Peter Bellamy. Never mind that it would satisfy the savage beast within him as well.

For a moment he paused at the starboard side and simply soaked in the breathtaking view of the silvery disk of the sun as it slipped into the rippling mocha waters.

The horizon gleamed like buttered rum. Golden glimmers tinged with red skipped over the waves as if they were ablaze, glimmers of light that matched the highlights in Kira's long luxurious hair.

Kira. Why did she bring out such poetic yearnings in him?

Out here was nothing but the sea, mistress to many of his ancestors. Mistress to him in many ways.

He shook his head at his own fanciful musings and took the stairs to the fly bridge. A stocky old sailor, wearing cutoff jeans and a tattered T-shirt, manned the helm.

"How's she sail, Captain?"

The old salt flashed him a cunning grin. "I'd ask the same

of you if I thought you'd tell me who that tempting gal is that you stowed on board."

André scowled. "It's a long story."

The Captain chuckled. "Most interesting ones are."

He shrugged. Though their friendship spanned a decade, he was loath to explain his association with Kira.

"Just keep it steady," André said. "The lady isn't accustomed to the sea."

"Aye, aye, boss."

André gave the horizon one last look, then hit the stairs. Annoyance bobbed within him like a storm-tossed buoy. Thanks to the scandal, every moment away from his desk cost him a fortune.

He hadn't intended to make any changes at the Chateau as yet, for he wanted Kira to squirm, to wonder what he planned to do, to get comfortable in her role as his lover. Then he'd swoop in and exert his will over the hotel—and her.

Oui, he'd not soften toward Kira. He would not make the same mistakes his father had made. No woman would rule *him*.

André slammed into the master stateroom and dropped onto a tufted leather chair at his desk, even though he ached to pace the confines like a caged tiger scenting fresh meat. He grabbed the phone and put in a call to his private detective. The man answered on the second ring.

"Is Bellamy still at the Chateau?" André asked, dispensing with pleasantries.

"No. He left an hour after you did."

"Back to Florida?"

"To California, to inaugurate a new hotel," he said. "Do you want me to continue surveillance?"

"*Oui*. I want to know every damned thing he does. Who he talks to, who he does business with."

"You got it," the detective said.

André ended the connection and rocked back in his chair, his mind sifting through this startling news. Why was Bellamy carrying on as if nothing had happened instead of rushing back to his compound in Florida? It didn't make sense, for Bellamy had seen André leave with Kira. The deception was over.

Had she simply been Bellamy's pawn, used to publicly humiliate André? Used as needed and then discarded? Paid off with shares in the Chateau? It was a possibility he'd considered.

His fight with Edouard had been personal, rife with emotions André deemed crippling. Simple revenge. He was David going up against Goliath.

His feud with Peter was strictly business. One corporate raider battling another. But over the last six months Bellamy had turned vicious. Personal attacks on André that the media fed on.

Where Edouard had regarded him as a pest, Peter Bellamy set out to destroy him. And Kira had sided with the enemy to bring about his ruin.

Yet he desired her.

Mon Dieu! Sleep deprivation was warping his mind. He rubbed his gritty eyes and winced. His body screamed for rest, yet he couldn't afford it yet.

André threw the pen on his desk and stormed from his stateroom. In moments he'd reached the main salon. His gaze sought and found the object of his scorn.

She lay curled on the sofa, napping, her hair spilling over a pillow in a waterfall of mahogany curls. He wasn't sure how she managed to look innocent and provocative at the same time. Nor could he understand why he wanted her, knowing she was a calculating liar.

But his pulse quickened all the same. He longed to run his fingers through her hair as he covered her body with his. Would she welcome his caresses? Melt in his embrace? Sigh as he thrust inside her?

He undid the knot in his tie and gave it a savage jerk. The silver-gray silk whistled free in the quiet. He'd know soon.

CHAPTER THREE

KIRA stirred, awakened by the crushed-velvet voice of her dreams. She understood very little French, but her body recognized the sultry promise his tone evoked.

She frowned, annoyed. It was always this way——André's voice rousing her from sleep as if to taunt her about the passion they'd shared once. Passion she'd never had with another man. Passion she missed with a soul-deep ache that never left her.

As always, she was helpless to stop the desire radiating in her belly, spreading low and leaving her hot and throbbing and so restless she couldn't lie still. She thrashed and arched in mute supplication for his touch, his kiss.

His hand glided under her skirt and up her inner thigh, his fingers splaying over her skin, so close to where she wept for his touch. Sensations exploded in her in dizzying colors and she moaned as she was drawn into the kaleidoscope of desire.

A soft laugh shattered the dream. She froze, knowing before her eyes popped open that the intimate touch was as real as the man. André loomed over her, his eyes dark and his features unreadable, his fingers inches from the juncture of her thighs.

Her heart careened crazily, for in that second she wanted him to touch her there like he had before. Wanted him to see her as a woman with dreams and hopes, not just as a sexual partner.

The knowledge that wouldn't likely happen snapped her from her sensual haze.

She slammed her hands against his shoulders. Mistake. Electricity arced into her as his muscles bunched and quivered. Her hands shifted over his chest, and she marveled at the power pulsing beneath her palms that she ached to explore.

"Stop it," she said, as much to herself as to him, shoving against him to scoot away, only to have the sofa's marble-topped divider table stop her. "What do you think you are doing?"

His lips pulled into a predatory smile that made her shiver with sexual awareness. "That should be obvious."

She shook her head, shocked he'd taken advantage of her while she was sleeping, stunned that she'd nearly begged him to take her. Hard. Fast. Deep.

"I'm not making that mistake again."

Something akin to pain flashed in his eyes, a lightning strike of emotion she couldn't read. "Yet you desire me, *oui?*"

"No."

"I know when a woman is faking and when she is gripped by passion."

One bold hot finger slipped beneath the lace trim of her silky panties and traced the sensitive crease of her leg. She couldn't stop the tremor that bolted through her, leaving her quivering with need.

She drew on every ounce of courage she possessed to defy his potent masculinity and preserve what remained of her dignity. "You're wrong. I don't want you."

André slid his finger from her, depriving her of his touch, giving her false security. He flashed a beautifully masculine smile and skimmed that same finger over the desire-dampened crotch of her panties.

Her body jerked of its own volition. She bit her lip to stifle a moan of raw pleasure, and her face flamed with embarrassment and anger for he'd proven his point.

She was putty in his hands. Helpless to resist him.

"I knew you were ready before I touched you," he said.

"André, don't," she said, curling her fingers into fists so she couldn't clutch him and draw him to her.

"Why? We have nothing to lose."

"You're wrong." She was already in danger of losing her heart to him—which made no sense, considering how he'd taken over her hotel and was dragging her to his island lair.

"Is that a challenge?" His hand slid down her calf and lower, sending hot quivers of sensation spiraling up her leg.

"No." She'd be a fool to square off against André when her defenses were so low, when she was so weary she could barely think straight.

He didn't play fair, and she did. Even now, with her emotions stretched thin, she became lost in his touch. Her breath hitched and her heart raced, and she willed his hand to glide back up her leg, to—

His palm cupped her foot, the fingers curling beneath the arch to skim the ball of her foot. A burning pain shot up her leg and her pleasure popped like a child's balloon.

"Don't! That hurts." An exaggeration. The skin burned hot all over.

He examined her foot, his frown darkening. His finger lightly traced the strap indentations cutting across her skin and she set her teeth against the fiery pinpricks that danced across her skin.

He spat out a torrent of French that she was sure were curses, yet his touch remained gentle. "You are a fool to sacrifice comfort for fashion. How long have your feet been like this?"

"They began hurting as we walked from the car to the dock."

"You should have told me."

She glared at him and tried pulling her foot free of his hold. "You were not exactly in a friendly mood."

He moved faster than lightning, pressing her deeper into the sumptuous cushions, blanketing her with his powerful body. His arms bracketed beside her head kept some of his weight off her, but not his groin. She felt the steely length of his sex against her belly and bit back a moan, afraid he'd ravish her, and equally afraid she'd not find the will to stop him.

"Discovering I had been tricked by my fiercest rival's mistress puts me in a bad mood," he said, his mouth tantalizingly close to hers, his eyes dark and mercurial.

"I'm not Peter's mistress," she said, willing him to believe her this time.

His features changed, hardening more than she'd thought was possible. "Why do you persist in lying?"

"Why won't you believe me?"

He snorted. "Because I know what you are."

Hot color stained her cheeks, her anger mounting. "No, you only think you do."

"Then tell me. How did you gain control of the Chateau?"

The truth was poised on her tongue, burning to be released. There was no reason to keep the promise she'd made Edouard. No reason except to weigh the danger in confiding in André. For if he hated her now, he'd despise her when he knew the rest.

"Having trouble sorting out your lies?" he asked.

No, the truth. "Nothing of the sort."

Kira looked away from the anger flashing in André's eyes. She was tired of working long hours to earn her rightful place at the Chateau, only to have a stranger step in and take it all away from her. Tired of living on the fringe of Edouard Bellamy's life so his family would be spared the stigma of knowing that he'd sired and provided for his bastard. Tired of receiving only crumbs of Edouard's affection. Tired of fighting this same argument with André.

"I'm simply an employee who invested wisely in Bellamy Enterprises," she said at last, repeating the excuse Edouard had devised.

"Did you receive a bonus when you came to my island and seduced me?"

"Of course not. I came to talk with you," she said.

"So you said. Yet you found your way into my bed."

"It was a mutual seduction."

"*Oui*, but I wasn't the one who invited the world to witness our affair the next morning."

Kira shook her head, having nothing to say in her defense. He wouldn't believe her anyway. She wouldn't rail at him, because he volleyed her barbs back with the ease of a tennis pro—only his shots drew blood.

"Neither did I."

"Perhaps you didn't issue the order," he said. "But you were aware that was Peter's intent before you came."

"If I had known, I assure you I'd never have come," she said, furious that he doubted her at every turn. "And, for the last time, my solicitor had assured me that you'd requested a meeting between us."

"Bravo, Miss Montgomery, for sticking with your story. Perhaps later you can entertain me with the story of how a new employee managed to buy a forty-nine percent holding in a multimillion-dollar Las Vegas hotel."

Before she could think how or if she should respond to that, a shrill whistle echoed in the salon.

He surged to his feet, his features rigid with anger. "We've arrived at Petit St. Marc."

Kira intended to do little more than rest for the remainder of this day, and maybe the next as well. She'd deal with André and the baby that tied them together later.

She watched him shrug into his suit jacket and give the lapels a tug. Except for the shadow of a beard lending him a roguish look, he looked no worse for wear.

Kira was sure she looked as weary as she felt. She swung her legs off the sofa and tugged down the skirt he'd rucked to her thighs. Her cheeks burned hot with mortification.

In London she'd spent her days working in a hotel and her evenings devoted to night classes. Edouard Bellamy had paid for her hospitality degree, but he'd insisted that was all the education she needed. She was, as her father had reminded her often, only suited to be a hospitality manager. But she'd had higher aspirations.

She needed a business degree to run a hotel. *Her* hotel!

Kira picked up her sling heels, hooked her purse over her shoulder and started across the main salon. The carpet felt good underfoot, but the onyx floors were sheer heaven, cooling her feverish feet like nothing else had.

No matter what else she did when she settled into a cottage, she intended to soak her abused feet. She descended the steps with care and moved across the carpeted deck to the railing. Her first look at the island took her breath away.

The lush rainforest on Petit St. Marc covered the humped dome of an extinct volcano. The knot of trees was so lush and dense that the forest appeared black at its heart—much like André's must surely be.

Palm trees close to the water swayed in the gentle southeasterly breeze that was refreshing her heated skin as it skipped over the expanse of sea, carrying with it the tang of salt and the intoxicating sweet scent of exotic flowers.

She tensed as his shadow fell over her, but as the island came into sharp focus her temper mellowed. "It's breathtaking."

"Oui," he said.

She looked away from the men mooring the yacht with quiet efficiency to André. Instead of staring at the island he frowned at her, as if he couldn't believe she'd seen beauty here. As if he couldn't believe she was here again.

Not by choice. And not for long, if she had anything to say about it.

"Come. The hour grows late." He motioned toward the short gangplank being secured to the aft deck.

Kira moved down it with care, and stepped onto the weathered boards of the dock. Heat burned the soles of her feet. She hissed in a breath and took a cautious step.

"Do you need help?" he asked.

"No. I just need to put on my shoes."

She gripped the railing and tried to don her slings. Impossible. Her feet were too swollen to fit under the straps.

Strong arms swept her off her feet.

She grabbed André's shoulders and felt a frisson of heat shoot through her. "You don't have to carry me."

"There is much I don't have to do, *ma chérie*." He carried her with effortless grace down the length of the dock.

Kira wanted to upbraid him for his Neanderthal ways, but she couldn't bring herself to knock his kindness. The closeness to him was to her detriment, though, for resting against the stalwart wall of his chest not only teased her with erotic memories, but incited the desire to create new ones.

Dangerous thoughts. Hopefully when she was in her own quarters she'd be able to control this bizarre attraction to André. She wasn't fool enough to believe she could remain indifferent to him.

André deposited her in the front seat of a canopied utility cart, his hands lingering on her bare skin for a charged fraction before deserting her. She tugged her skirt over her knees, annoyed that her body still throbbed with desire.

The utility cart dipped slightly as he eased his big frame behind the wheel, power and sensuality radiating off him in waves that rivaled the golden-tinged ones rolling toward the shore. He'd removed his jacket and rolled up his shirtsleeves, revealing tanned forearms corded with muscle and sprinkled with black hair. The breeze flattened his fine shirt against the hard planes of his chest and upper arms.

He was all power and dominance, a king in his kingdom. But it was that sultry gleam in his eyes as they undressed her that took her breath away. For just one look had her forgetting about the tenuous position she was in.

Disgusted at her weakness for him, she turned her head to watch a young Carib jostle her luggage onto the rear deck of the cart. Unlike his decadently rich employer's, his smile was kind and respectful.

Kira returned the gesture. Though the Caribs treated her like a guest, she suspected none of them would help her escape.

What unnerved her was that her captivity was two-fold. For the child growing within her bound her tighter to André than any lock or key.

The vehicle jolted forward, the electric hum of its engine fading as the peaceful sigh of the island took dominance. "Do you ever grow weary of it here?"

"Only during hurricane season."

He maneuvered the utility cart up a winding path paved with crushed seashells, the fat tires crunching them into a finer roadbed. The smooth surface was a welcome surprise.

Kira scanned the area anew. The first time she'd come here she'd been too incensed to appreciate the resort. And now? Her gaze took in the red-tiled roofs of the cottages almost hidden in the forest, and moved down to the secluded white beach below.

She caught a glimpse of a couple strolling hand in hand, naked as the day they were born. "You have a nude beach here?"

"Four natural beaches, all private, and all reserved beforehand by the guests." A hint of a smile touched his mouth. "Tops are optional on the public beach. We are very European here."

"I'm too British to appreciate it."

"You'll learn to enjoy it."

Never. Unlike her mother, she didn't flaunt her body.

Kira closed her eyes to the beauty around her as the ugliness of her past tried to intrude. No, she wasn't like her mother at all. She slid a hand over her belly. The past was just that—past. This baby was her future.

The utility vehicle whirred past another lane leading to another cottage and sped up an incline beneath a canopy of trees alive with birds. Through the light flickering through the foliage Kira caught a glimpse of the big house, nestled into the hillside.

She gripped the handrail and swallowed the panic building in her chest. He *couldn't* mean to move her into his dwelling.

But as the vehicle emerged from the trees into an area

cleared behind the old plantation house, she was certain that was his intention. Living on his island would be taxing enough. But to stay in his home and endure his temper? Impossible.

"I'd prefer my own quarters." Away from him and temptation.

"The cottages are for paying guests." He stepped from the cart and pocketed the key.

"Fine. I'll pay," she said, craning her neck to see where he'd gone. "I won't live with you."

"You don't have a choice, *ma chérie*."

She whipped around to find him at her side. One arm rested on the top of the canopy and the other gripped the support pole.

At first glance his was a casual pose. But one look at his white knuckles, at the corded muscles in his arms and the grim set of his mouth, dispelled that thought.

"I won't be your mistress," she said.

"I didn't offer you the position."

It was true. He hadn't said a word about her being his lover. She should feel relieved, not disappointed. What was wrong with her?

His enigmatic gaze held hers another long moment before he straightened and extended a hand to her. "It has been a taxing journey. Come. I'll help you inside."

"I can manage myself." Kira swung her legs out and stood.

Her sensitive feet settled onto the crushed shells and her breath hitched, but she was determined to walk into his house under her own power.

"Mon Dieu!" André stepped forward and swept her up in his arms again. "Are you always this stubborn?"

She planted her hands on his shoulders to force a minute distance between their bodies. "Are you always this domineering?"

"Only with you."

Kira didn't believe that for a moment as he strode up the walk, his shoes crunching the walkway. She resisted the urge to rest her head against his shoulder, refused to relax against the comforting wall of his chest.

He climbed the two steps to the front terrace with ease. The temperature was refreshingly cooler beneath the roofed porch. His housekeeper stood at the open door, the white ruffle on her peasant blouse and the hem of her orange floral skirt fluttering in the breeze that filtered through the house.

A smile wreathed her face. "*Bonjour*, Monsieur Gauthier."

"*Bon après-midi*, Otillie." André shouldered through the door with Kira in his arms, speaking rapidly in the island patois which sailed right over Kira's head.

Otillie volleyed back with what sounded like affronted questions, and stepped in front of André, bringing him up short.

After a few choice words from him, Otillie tossed her hands in the air and quit the living room, muttering under her breath.

"What was that about?" Kira asked.

"Otillie is annoyed with me for not telling her I was bringing a guest home."

"You should have let me rent a cottage."

"I should have kicked you off my island when you first came here to play out your vengeance."

"Why didn't you?" she asked, refusing to be baited into the same argument about her reasons for coming here.

"Because you intrigued me."

That feeling had been mutual. She'd never met a man like André. Never felt such a strong connection to another man. It had been more than sex to her, yet she suspected that was where their similarities ended.

He climbed the steps with apparent ease and continued down a hall swathed in shadows. Her blood heated and her heart quickened, for she knew there were only bedrooms on this level.

And she knew exactly which room was his.

Tingles of awareness streaked through her, sending her heart into a crazy rhythm. Was that where he was taking her? Would she be a prisoner in his bed?

Surely not? Even André couldn't be that barbarous. Yet he'd taken her from the Chateau and brought her here. She was on his island. In his house. At his mercy.

Mercy? She gave in to a shiver. He had none.

He was a ruthless corporate pirate and a master of seduction. She might not be a match for him in business, but she'd proved she was his carnal equal. In that they were well suited.

That admission terrified her more than anything, for she was fatally attracted to him—like a moth to a flame. She'd been burned once by tumbling into his bed. The next time the flames of desire would consume her—if his quest for vengeance didn't destroy her first.

He passed the door to his chamber without pause—the room where they'd made love, the room where the world had intruded on their ideal, the room she'd fled in anger and shame.

She shook off those memories as he shouldered open a louvered door midway down the hall, and pushed into a cool, dark room. A gorgeous canopied bed dominated the space, its mosquito netting rippling in the refreshing breeze that filtered through the room.

André headed straight toward the bed, his features so hard and unyielding they looked carved from stone. Yet he laid her on the bed gently, his touch lingering a telling moment.

Instead of pouncing on her, as she'd half expected he'd do, he stood back and stared at her with cold derision. She sensed he waged a war within himself, and a part of her commiserated, for she was fighting her own private battle to remain unmoved by him. It had been so good between them that one glorious night.

Though her heart pounded louder than the drums that had greeted them on their arrival, she sat up and faced him. And waited for him to break the tense silence.

"I'm a private man," he said, pacing before the foot of the bed. "I guarded my business and my private life. But in one night you stripped me bare and invited the world as witness."

"I had nothing to do with that swarm of paparazzi."

He sliced a hand through the air. "Of course you *would* deny your part in that."

"What about you?" she asked, having learned after Edouard's death that André wasn't a man to be crossed—or trusted. "You're as much to blame for the dissolution of your engagement."

He released a cold, hard laugh. "As much as I value privacy, my former fiancée cherished it more. You destroyed that and humiliated her."

"I didn't do it alone," she said, in a burst of irritation.

He slammed both hands on the footboard, making the bed shake. "Don't remind me."

His eyes burned into hers, a mixture of anger and desire that made her light-headed. She looked away, breaking the spell.

At least André was no longer in the limelight. Just two weeks ago, a new celebrity upheaval had dimmed the spotlight on André Gauthier and his equally rich ex-fiancée. And the hunt to find his mystery lover—Kira—had finally lost its appeal.

But Kira would always regret being "the other woman"—a role she'd vowed never to assume. "I'm sorry your fiancée was hurt."

"Are you?" he asked.

"Yes! I'm not a homewrecker. If I'd known you were engaged I never would have let you touch me."

"But of course you have manipulated this in your mind, so I am to blame for not telling you."

"Why didn't you speak up?"

An awful quiet hummed between them. The muscles and tendons in his face were stretched so tight she feared they'd snap. He looked angry enough to kill her with his bare hands, and at that moment she wouldn't have blamed him.

She was furious at herself for listening to her solicitor and coming here for the meeting that André had always denied requesting. Though they'd tumbled into bed soon after, he surely had to admit he was as much at fault as her—maybe more so.

For he'd been affianced. He should have sent Kira away instead of seducing her.

"Do you have any idea what you did to me?" he asked, his voice lethally soft.

She bit back the desire to ask him the same, for that would lead to questions she wasn't prepared to answer yet. "I exposed you for what you are. It was you alone who broke her heart."

"Are you really that naïve?"

Anger sparked in her—again directed as much at herself as at him. "I know what I saw. When your fiancée found us together she was devastated that you'd broken your pledge to her. If she hadn't loved you, your infidelity wouldn't have bothered her."

He shook his head and his mouth pulled into a grim smile. "*Oui*, she was furious that my affair was made public. So furious she rescinded the offer that would have merged our companies. You, Miss Montgomery, cost me a fortune."

Kira blanched, certain he was exaggerating. "You make it sound as if your impending marriage was just a business merger."

"It was."

"You can't be serious."

"But I am. You did more than create a scandal," he said. "You interfered in a lucrative deal. But then Peter must have made you aware of that. That's why you must suffer the consequences of your actions."

That was why he'd struck now to acquire the Chateau—why he'd blackmailed her into leaving with him. The corporate raider with meticulous timing. The father of her child.

A man who broke his vows—just like her father. A man who took pleasure exacting revenge.

Without another word he turned and stormed from the room, closing the door behind him with a demoralizing click.

Kira leapt from the bed and raced to the door, not done with this argument yet. She spied his shadow through the louvers and grabbed the knob, but it wouldn't turn. Locked.

She pounded the doorframe so hard the louvers rattled. "Unlock this door! We need to talk."

"I've said all I intend to say for now."

"Wait! You can't keep me in here."

"*Oui*, I can."

It was a fact she detested. She was marooned on an island with a man who burned with revenge—and she was pregnant with his child. He likely believed he'd rendered her helpless.

But then, André really didn't know her.

"If you don't unlock this door, I'll—I'll—"

"Do what?" he asked, his voice smug. "Throw a tantrum?"

Kira seethed and scanned the room. Her gaze fell on a pair of rococo vases adorning a shelf. Old Paris Mantle vases, she was sure. Lovely. Delicate.

"No, something far more valuable," she said, and heaved both vases at the door. The porcelain shattered in a million rose-hued shards—just like her dreams.

CHAPTER FOUR

ANDRÉ stood in the hall, chest heaving and fists shaking at his sides. He'd not intended to lock her in her room, but the moment he'd held her in his arms and kissed her he'd wanted her so badly he throbbed with need. Knowing she was receptive to him only made the urge to possess her again stronger than ever.

So he'd locked the door to keep her from charging from the room and challenging him. For this time he'd not be able to walk away. It was a chilling admission to make.

He'd never experienced this sensual intensity with another woman. He'd soared to a summit with Kira that he'd not known existed. A place he'd feared going all his life, for he'd had to relinquish control to get there.

It had been just one night of passion. One damned night. But he recalled every detail. The taste of her skin, the silken strength of her muscles straining with his, her lusty response to each intimate stroke of his hands, his mouth, his body.

Mon Dieu, her anger was as fiery as her desire—the flint to ignite his passion. Knowing she'd flung a set of exquisite rococo vases against the door had awakened a primitive side in him. Like the passion-crazed hero in *La Valse Chaloupée*, he was tempted to kick down the door, grab her by her hair, and drag her into his bedroom.

But this was life, not a facsimile of the Apache Dance.

Though he was his father's only son, he'd be damned if he'd let a woman blind him to reason. Not again!

History would not repeat itself through him. Never.

Yet it had, for he'd been lenient with her from the start. That would end now.

Though Kira was the object of his baser desires, she'd been his enemy's mistress. She'd come here to seduce him, to drag his name through the muck. Her success had ruined the most lucrative deal of his life, and made a fool of him.

His enemy had won that battle through her. But he'd not be deterred from his goal this time.

Biting off a curse, he strode the length of the hall to his room. The southeasterly breeze drifting through his chamber failed to refresh him.

He was weary and hot, and disgusted with himself. Spending the better part of a day in Kira's close company had driven him mad with lust.

André strode into his *en suite* glass-enclosed shower and turned the jets on full blast. Cold water rained down on his body, pelting muscles that had grown so tense and knotted they ached.

He flattened both hands on the ceramic-tiled wall and put down his head, welcoming the water coursing over his body, cooling his ardor, his anger. The intense feelings warring within him were new, and he hated that he'd lost control with her again.

Yes, this had to be similar to the hell his father had endured throughout his marriage. André would have none of it.

The water spurting from the jets beat his savage jealousy for Kira to a manageable level. He'd run on pure adrenaline the past few hours. But he'd accomplished what he'd set out to do.

He'd brought Kira to Petit St. Marc and he'd exact his revenge. Peter Bellamy would be livid by now, knowing that he held Kira here, that he'd use whatever means necessary to access any secrets she held about Bellamy Enterprises. Yet Bellamy had been deceptively silent, going about his life as if nothing out of the ordinary had happened. What was his plan?

Perhaps Bellamy had anticipated André would strike back, that he'd go after Kira to bring Bellamy to heel? Perhaps that was why Kira hadn't put up much resistance to leave the Chateau. Perhaps the plan was to ensure that lightning struck twice—she was to seduce him and create another media nightmare.

It was a possibility he couldn't ignore. Paparazzi could be on their way to the island now, in hopes of catching André availing himself of Bellamy's tempting mistress again.

The thought pulsed in his blood like lava, thick and scalding hot.

André pushed away from the shower wall and turned off the water. The cold dousing had cooled his temper, but he was still semi-aroused.

He stalked into his room, his body dripping water, his sex heavy. He stared at the security panel, smiled, then punched in numbers to deactivate the lock on her door.

Bellamy's feigned uninterest in André taking Kira from the Chateau roused his darkest suspicions. If she made no attempt to escape, then it was likely she and Bellamy already had an ulterior plan in place, should André try to use Kira to crush Bellamy.

He wouldn't be played for a fool again. He'd alerted his guards to bar anyone except their guests from the island. He'd set men to patrol the shoreline as well, for the same reason.

New game. New rules. One winner—him.

Kira pressed one hand to the *en suite* bathroom door while the other tightened around the knob, her pulse racing with a sense of dread and anticipation. She'd just decided she might as well take a shower to cool her anger when she'd heard the lock on her door click. But she hadn't heard the door open.

She strained to hear, but the only sound she detected was the soft whir of the ceiling fan and the pounding of her own heart. André must have returned.

Good. She was ready to confront him, for the longer she put this off the worse it would be. Or was it already too late?

She pressed a hand over her still-flat belly, her emotions more tangled than before, her anger cooling. André believed she was Peter's mistress. Believed she'd come to the island before to ruin him. Believed she was his enemy.

Kira could produce a document to debunk that claim. But, short of a DNA test, she feared she'd never convince André of his paternity. Not unless she earned his trust first.

Taking a resigned breath, she opened the bathroom door and stepped into the room. A glance proved she was the only one in residence. She eased to the entrance door and peeked through the louvers.

Her brow creased. No masculine shadow in the hall.

Yet someone had thrown open the heavy curtains in the hall and opened the windows to let the refreshing ocean breeze riffle in. She strained to hear sounds of life, and caught a faint murmur of voices echoing from below stairs.

Kira closed her door and paced the luxurious bedroom. Why had he locked her in, only to set her free soon afterward? Why had he left her in peace?

Peace? That was a laugh.

There'd be no peace until she and André came to amiable terms regarding their child. Though, considering who she was, it was likely he'd regard her with hate. And what of their child?

Surely the island tycoon who'd loved her to distraction wasn't as cold as her own father? André would insist on playing a vital role in their child's life. And hers as well?

If she was honest with herself, she wanted the fairy tale dream of a loving husband and family.

She wanted André.

This dangerous fascination she had with him made no sense to her. He was all wrong for her. She detested his infidelity. His arrogance. His ruthless intention to take what he wanted without a care for her feelings.

He believed she was Peter's mistress—his enemy. What did he intend to do with her? What would he do when he learned the whole truth?

Restless energy pulsed within her, leaving her thoughts scrambled and her stomach alive with butterflies. She crossed to the window, where cream voile curtains fluttered like gossamer wings.

The vista was a feast: sky bathed in the richest bronze and edged in an ethereal glow. Like André's tanned skin, smooth, unblemished, potently sensual.

She frowned, annoyed she couldn't enjoy a pastoral thought without him crowding into her mind. Like a thorn, André Gauthier was embedded in her, festering, painful when poked.

Her hand stole to her belly and her eyes stung with tears she refused to shed. André was in her, his blood coursing in their child, mixing with hers. The child bound them together. But what would the future hold for them all? Could they find a way to resolve their differences for the baby's sake?

Kira shook her head, apprehensive and weary. She'd worked so hard to gain confidence in herself, yet in less than a day he'd rendered her poise nonexistent.

He was too dominant.

Too virile.

Too addictive to her senses.

She didn't want to want him. Didn't want to think of him. Yet he remained constant in her mind. He kept her worries alive, churning like a whirlpool.

She needed to unwind, to work off the tension coiling and striking like maddened vipers within her. Because as long as her emotions were this frayed, she remained vulnerable to André.

Around the plantation house the rainforest had been cut back to allow a garden paradise. Lanterns outlined the fence, and more strategically placed lights spotlighted fabulous floral displays.

Nearly in the center lay a large swimming pool, awash in

soft light. Several small thatched shelters strung with inviting hammocks stood nearby, the encroaching shadows of dusk lending them more privacy.

The pool beckoned to her. She licked her lips, debating.

Nothing had been said regarding an evening meal, though she caught a tantalizing spicy aroma drifting from below. She didn't know if she was expected to dine with André or eat alone in her room. She wasn't sure of anything. But she reasoned she had time for a quick dip in the pool.

Kira dug through her luggage and found her simple coral maillot. In another month her pregnancy would make her hesitant to wear anything this revealing. So she might as well enjoy this opportunity while she could.

Once she'd donned her swimsuit, she stood in front of the mirror and critically studied herself. She wasn't showing yet. Still she hesitated, until she'd borrowed a large bath towel. She wrapped it sari-fashion around her and slipped from the room.

For a moment she stood there, listening, afraid André would appear. Or worse. That he'd take her in his arms. Kiss her. Melt her resolve.

But not a soul stirred, and the quiet bolstered her flagging courage. She hurried across the cool beechwood floors to the stairs. Again she paused, listening, heart hammering.

Nobody was about, so she padded down the steps and hurried to French doors thrown open to welcome the prevailing breezes. She stepped onto a terrace facing the forest and breathed in the exotic perfume of flowers.

The lights lent a fantasy glow to the garden, and in no time she'd padded down the terracotta stones to the pool. It seemed too good to be true that this enchanted garden was all hers to enjoy this evening.

Kira undid the towel at her waist and let it drop, then stepped to the deep end of the pool and dived into its turquoise depth. The water was almost too warm and drugging, but she forced her arms to slice through the water, her legs to scissor and propel her across the pool.

One lap and turn. Then two, three, four…

She stopped counting after that. Though she was tired to her core, the repetition was the nirvana she sought to banish André from her mind.

André watched the monitor, transfixed by the woman cleanly navigating his Olympic-sized pool. He'd not taken time to study her body impartially. If he had, he'd have recognized she possessed an athlete's physique.

Her sleek suit was designed to minimize drag. It molded to her and left nothing for the imagination. Not that he needed to guess what was beneath the suit.

He remembered every nuance of her body. Every curve, every dimple, right down to the sexy mole on her derrière.

Yet his research into Kira Montgomery had failed to tell him she was an expert swimmer. Not a leisurely one either. No, she swam with speed and power, the defined muscles in her arms and shoulders attesting that she was fit. That she was a competitor.

He smiled, pleased to discover a reason for the aggressive tendency which had drawn him to her. Though he could see she was used to challenging others in the pool, she was far out of her league in trying to best him.

He was a shark, whereas she was a sleek dolphin. Graceful, swift and desirable. Cunning as well?

Heat pooled in his groin as he watched her slice through the water, over and over. A sea nymph come to life, luring him to come to her. That was likely her plan   to seduce him again.

But this time he was alert to her scheme. This time he'd use her own desire against her. This time he'd turn the tables on her.

He pushed from his chair and strode from the room, the cutoff jeans he'd donned barely clinging to his hips, his chest and feet as bare as his rising need.

With Bellamy's help she'd succeeded in breaching his

defenses. His lust for her had eroded his control, for he'd never been so attracted to a woman before. Never enjoyed such sensual sparring.

But he'd not make the same mistake twice. This time he was aware of the depth of her deceit.

Oui, when he was done with Kira Montgomery she'd be financially ruined and humiliated. As for her benefactor—he'd strip Peter Bellamy of his fortune and his empire.

Only then would his revenge be complete.

Kira felt the pressure of water swelling behind her, followed by the tingling sensation that she wasn't alone. She faltered midway to glance back at the tiled edge.

She recognized the circle of ripples for what they were—someone had dived in. André?

The thought of him in the pool with her drugged her limbs and muddled her thoughts. It had to be him, for even the water was charged with an energy that hadn't been there before.

Kira went hot and cold and hot again, her heart drumming too fast. She pulled herself through the water, determined to outdistance André. She found a burst of renewed speed and concentrated on reaching the far wall before him.

She had to get out of the water. She had to be on firm ground when she encountered him again.

Doing laps had cleared her head, and she was glad she hadn't blurted out the truth earlier. He was too mired in anger to reason with, too set on seducing her out of some misguided sense of revenge to deal with the reality of their future.

There would be time later to explain everything. She'd make time. She'd somehow make him understand that she'd played no part in Peter Bellamy's schemes. That she was the injured party in this—just like him.

That, despite the feud between the Bellamys and André, they'd created something beautiful together. That they had a chance for a bright future.

But now wasn't the time to discuss it. The day had exhausted her and strained his patience.

Tomorrow. She'd deal with all this then.

Her arms sliced the water with precision, her shoulders burning from the exertion, her thighs growing tighter, her lungs starting to burn.

The intricate mosaic design on the tile edging the far end of the pool became clearer, the bright red, blue and yellow more intense. Almost there. Almost.

She felt the pressure of water pushing at her from below. Panic nipped at her, for she knew he was a heartbeat away from colliding with her.

A great white shark chasing her, poised to attack. She chanced a look down, faltering when she saw him.

His long powerful body surged upward to meld with hers, his hands on her waist anchoring her to him. Before she could think to fight him, he broke the water and shot upward, taking her with him.

The night breeze whispered over her body, pebbling her skin. She slammed both palms on his wet chest to push him away, but the raw hunger in his eyes paralyzed her.

He smiled, arrogant and potently sexy. Then his mouth captured hers and she surrendered with a whimper.

They fell back into the water, the splash noisy and ungraceful. Her hands slipped around his neck, her fingers memorizing the play of muscle flexing beneath warm smooth skin.

She'd missed this connection to him so much.

The water lapped over them as they sank in the pool, and she clung to him. The kiss deepened, breathing life into her.

He was her anchor and her damnation. As before, his kiss was unlike any she'd experienced. Deep, wild, intoxicating, dragging her through hell to glimpse heaven.

Each glide of skin against skin sent shockwaves of need vibrating through her, crumbling the walls of restraint she'd hastily erected. Just like that and she capitulated to him.

There was no reason to continue fighting when he'd won this battle. She wanted him, and she hated herself for being so weak around him, hated this intense need that coursed in her for him.

With just a kiss he'd reduced her world to her and him and the child in her womb, nestled between them. But he didn't know that, or realize her concern at holding her breath too long.

He pushed off the bottom of the pool and propelled them upward. Toward air.

And another confrontation with André.

He held majority shares in her hotel as tightly as he held her life in his hands. She should fear him. But she believed that he'd protect her, even though her intuition warned she'd come out the loser in any personal war with him. Even knowing the danger ahead of her, she let him woo her heart without effort.

They broke the surface, each dragging in air—another form of torture, for her breasts rubbed his chest with each indrawn breath, teasing the nipples into aching peaks. And lower his sex pressed against her belly, separated only by her swimsuit.

A languid heat coiled in her at knowing he was naked. Knowing that it would be so simple to reach down and stroke his exquisite length, to guide him where she ached for him.

"You're an expert swimmer," he said, forcing her mind from sex—a blessing that part of her cursed.

"It's good exercise." No longer a passion.

Her dream to compete in watersports had died long ago, derailed by an injury, then later crushed beneath Edouard's plans for her.

She'd not relinquish another dream to please a man, no matter how much she ached for his touch, his possession. Yet even as the thought crossed her mind she admitted that was a lie. She ached to have a family. To be wanted. Loved.

He moved, lifting her to nuzzle her breasts through the thin Spandex of her swimsuit. Fire shot through her. She dug her fingers into his strong wet shoulders, trembling and arching her back to press her bosom closer to his mouth.

"I want you," he said, his teeth grazing one sensitized nipple before moving to the other. "You want me."

She moaned, awash in need, refusing to fight what they both wanted. "That's obvious."

He scowled, as if angered by her admission. "I won't take you now."

Had she heard him wrong? No, even as he spoke with biting conviction he pulled away from her, putting her at arm's length, slamming the door on the hot emotions she'd seen flickering in his eyes.

"Then why the foreplay?" she asked, disgusted that her face was flushed and her body trembled with desire.

"I was ravenous for an appetizer." He left her standing in the water and strode to the edge. "We will indulge in the sensual entrée later."

He hoisted himself from the pool, water sluicing down his naked and aroused body. He was tanned all over, though a slightly lighter hue banded his groin and his firm, sexy behind, indicating he wore a brief swimsuit on occasion.

The sight of his magnificent body intensified the ache in her. "I won't have sex with you."

"*Oui*, you will. But tonight I need rest and I need food." His gaze slid over her with a hunger that made her breath catch. "When we make love it will be leisurely and very thorough."

She trembled at the promise, at a loss as to what to say that wouldn't betray her wants, her needs.

"Dinner will be served in fifteen minutes," he said. "We'll dine casually tonight."

He stepped into his cutoff jean shorts, but left them unbuttoned, clinging to him like she longed to do. Then he walked away, his long strides taking him further from her. Just like that he could shut off his need for her, while she still quivered with want.

Damn him!

Kira slapped both palms on the calm water as anger danced

up her limbs. He didn't look back once, didn't pause. He stepped onto the terrace and into the house.

Frustrated beyond words, she launched into a breaststroke that took her the length of the pool and back. Yet even though her muscles screamed for rest as she climbed from the water, a part of her was still ravenous for André's touch.

She had to gain control of her emotions and her libido. For if she wasn't very careful her weakness for him would be the downfall from which she'd never recover.

After a quick shower, Kira donned a simple sundress patterned in aqua and a rich brown the color of André's eyes. That she could make the comparison confirmed she was still on dangerous ground around him. It didn't help that her emotions swung wildly due to her pregnancy.

One moment she hated him, the next she craved his touch, his kiss. She'd even pondered engaging him in a debate, but quelled the urge. Their first and last verbal clash had led them straight to the bedroom.

Considering how she'd melted in his arms in the pool, she dreaded sitting across from him at the dinner table. But her fears were for naught. Soon after they'd sat down to dine and their meal had been served, André was called away—an urgent conference call he must take.

Alarm bubbled in her. Her first fear was he'd made good on his threat to destroy her hotel. "If this concerns the Chateau—"

"It doesn't." He drained his glass of wine, his features remote. "Enjoy your meal, Miss Montgomery."

Without a backward glance, he strode from the room. His plate remained untouched.

Worry nipped along Kira's nerves, leaving her edgy. She didn't trust André to tell her the truth, for he was convinced that she was in league with Peter Bellamy.

He swore he had proof. So what did he have that condemned her? Or was it a bluff?

She speared a wedge of orange and trailed it through her serving of chicken, tomato and pepper and into a bed of wild rice. The subtle aroma of garlic and citrus that had appealed earlier deserted her. Yet she knew that she must eat something for the baby's sake.

She forced herself to eat and let her mind roam. What electronic proof could he have that tied her to Peter Bellamy?

It couldn't be genuine. So who'd manufactured this proof?

There were those at the Chateau who disliked her. Since she'd taken over things had gone awry. Items she'd needed hadn't been ordered. Reservations were often jumbled.

But even if one of them took their dislike of her beyond reasonable in an attempt to ruin her, nobody there had the power to sell Edouard Bellamy's shares.

No one except Peter. Edouard's son. He'd been made executor of Edouard's will. He'd inherited his father's corporation. Had *he* set out to strip her of her inheritance?

She dropped her fork on her plate and rubbed her aching temples. It was very possible that he'd discovered the role she'd played in Edouard's life. That Peter resented her with a towering hatred—just as Edouard had predicted would happen should the truth ever come out.

Everything had been a jumble since the accident. Edouard had clung to life while his mistress had lost hers. The dissolution of her stock had been swift and secretive, with André buying those shares in the Chateau.

That was what had sent Kira here to confer with André. A meeting André swore he'd never agreed to. Had she been set up from the start?

André believed she'd conspired with Peter to ruin him. Not true, but she had no idea how to prove her innocence. She didn't know what to do, who to trust beyond Claude, her solicitor.

Kira slumped back in her chair, her appetite and what little remained of her energy gone. She wanted to crawl in bed and sleep. Wanted to forget this nightmare that had become her life.

Her hand stole over her belly and, despite her annoyance and fears and worries, she smiled. More than anything she wanted to protect her baby. The best way to do that was rest.

She put her napkin on the table and rose. Her gaze collided with André's.

As before, his stance was deceptively casual as he leaned a shoulder against the doorjamb, arms hanging loose at his sides and one foot crossed over an ankle.

But his expression was dark and forbidding, and censure burned in his eyes. He was angry, and she wondered if that ire was the result of his conference call or with her.

"How long have you been there?" she asked.

"Long enough. You didn't eat enough to keep a bird alive."

"It's enough for now."

He snorted. "But of course you must ensure your figure remains desirable, *oui*?"

His handsome face had graced many a business magazine, but she'd only seen this ferocious expression once before. Three months ago, when she'd fled Petit St. Marc.

So much had happened, so quickly. It seemed surreal that she'd gone from being the hospitality manager at Edouard Bellamy's elite Le Cygne Hotel in London to stockholder of Chateau Mystique to André's impromptu lover.

But that seemed a lifetime ago.

Now fury ruled his features. From the rigid set of his lean jaw to the grim slash of his firm full lips. As ruthless as he'd seemed when she'd escaped the island, he appeared menacing now, like a bloodthirsty pirate instead of a renowned island tycoon.

Whatever had taken him away tonight had put him in a dangerous mood. But she was too tired and emotionally spent to spar with him tonight.

Still she asked, "Is something wrong?"

He shrugged, but his body remained tense. Wary. "My guards intercepted paparazzi off the coast."

"That should please you," she said, suspecting that diverting the media was a common occurrence on the island.

He pushed away from the doorjamb and prowled the room, like a predator stalking its prey. "What is he paying you to continue this charade?"

She gave a brittle laugh. "Am I to assume you mean Peter again? Because, if so, the answer is the same as before. I've never met Peter Bellamy, and I've never taken any directives from him."

"*Oui*, just from Edouard. He selected well when he chose you for his son," he said, and she debated lobbing the water carafe at his arrogant head.

"Why do you hate him?" she asked, thinking she should know what drove André before she said anything more. Certainly before she divulged her secret.

"Why?" André released a caustic laugh, his features devoid of humor. "Edouard Bellamy destroyed my family."

A sickening chill swept over Kira. "That's why you engineered the takeover of the Chateau? Why you want to break Bellamy Enterprises?"

"Revenge, *ma chérie*."

"But Edouard's dead."

His smile was so cold she felt as if she'd been plunged in ice water. "You are familiar with the concept of the sins of the father being visited upon his children, *oui*?"

Kira managed a weak nod, though her knees nearly buckled. "What has Peter done to you?"

Again the negligent shrug. "He's a Bellamy."

And that answer said it all. For she was a Bellamy as well, Edouard's daughter. And her baby—their baby!—had Bellamy blood.

She had to escape Petit St. Marc before he discovered the truth—before his vendetta against the Bellamys destroyed her and their child.

CHAPTER FIVE

ANDRÉ watched Kira. The skin at his nape was hot, his muscles bunched to spring forward and catch her should she faint. It seemed imminent. She swayed slightly and her face was leached of color again. All because he'd told her that he intended to destroy Edouard Bellamy's empire.

"It's been a trying day," she said at last, her voice strained and tinged with weariness. "I need sleep."

So did he, but he was too livid at his investigator's initial report to shut off his mind. "I have just discovered that Edouard Bellamy paid for your education and your efficient Mini Cooper car. And how interesting that you moved into the spacious flat that Peter had called home for over a year."

"You had me investigated?" she asked, features suddenly tense and expressive eyes wary.

"*Oui.*" She was the product of a single parent, and raised in an elite boarding school. Illegitimate, with "father unknown" marked on her birth certificate. "Bellamy gave you your first job as the hospitality manager at Le Cygne. Were you Peter's mistress by then?"

An angry red flush mottled her cheeks. "No! Edouard offered me a scholarship to further my education, but I landed that position at Le Cygne because of my high marks. I had no idea that his son had once lived in the flat I was lent."

He didn't believe that for a heartbeat. "What did you do to acquire forty-nine percent of Chateau Mystique?"

"We've been over this once—which was quite enough. Nothing has changed. Nothing *will* change. Because I've never been any man's mistress!"

She whirled toward the door and stumbled. He caught her, alarmed by her too-pale complexion and near faint.

"You should have eaten more," he said.

"It wouldn't stay down."

His brows slammed together. "You're ill? Should I send for a physician?"

"No, I'm just tired and thirsty. The doctor stressed I need to drink more fluid in my condi—" She broke off, her lips parting and her eyes going wide. It was the look of someone who'd said more than they'd intended.

His gaze narrowed on hers, his heart beating too fast as his mind found the only appropriate word to finish her thought. "What is your condition?"

She swallowed hard, her gaze locking on his. "I'm three months pregnant."

Mon Dieu! He drove his fingers through his hair, his mind reeling with that news. Had he known, had he suspected, he never would have taken her from the Chateau.

"But of course—you are *enceinte* with Peter's child."

"No, I'm not," she said, jerking free of him. "You are the father."

It was a lie. It had to be. But even as he thought it his mind replayed a vivid image of the one time he'd neglected to use protection. He'd wanted Kira so much that he'd not even thought about birth control until after the fact.

Now he would pay for that consequence. If it were true.

"When did you plan to tell me, *ma chérie*?"

She shook her head, hating that she'd blurted out the truth. But at least that secret was out. "I hadn't decided."

"Convenient." His gaze narrowed on her. "Was this part of

Bellamy's scheme to further smear my reputation, or your ticket to gain a greater fortune?"

Kira stared into dark angry eyes that flashed as fierce as the desert lightning storms that terrified her. She was crushed he believed her so mercenary. But she couldn't—wouldn't—explain herself, for she'd only incur his wrath.

"Answer me! Whose idea was it to steal my heir?"

A glint of longing softened his features, so brief she wondered if she'd imagined it, so real she nearly spoke with her heart. But no, it was too soon to trust him without question—never mind that she longed to do just that.

She'd been an unwanted child, disowned by her mother and regarded as an obligation by her father. She wouldn't let her child be treated so dispassionately by a rich father.

"Your heir?" She forced a laugh, the sound harsh to her own ears. "Is that all our child means to you?"

How dared she ask that? André's jaw throbbed from clenching his teeth. "There are tests that will prove if the baby you carry is your lover's or—"

"I won't risk my child's life to satisfy your curiosity," she said, a hand pressed protectively to her belly.

His temper flared. "*Mon Dieu*, do you think I'd put the baby's life at risk?"

"I don't know. You've done nothing to earn my trust."

"*Touché.*"

André ran a hand over the stubble on his jaw, damning the tremor streaking up his arm. The baby was likely Bellamy's.

But it was possible the child was his.

"My baby's health is more important than anything," she said, and he silently agreed with her. "Let me return to the Chateau. I need to see my doctor regularly—"

"I will arrange for an obstetrician from Martinique to visit you weekly here on Petit St. Marc."

"Weekly? You can't mean to keep me here."

"*Oui*, you will stay on the island for the duration of your pregnancy."

Until paternity could be proved, Kira realized with renewed annoyance.

Petit St. Marc would be her prison for the next six months. Unless she could break through the wall of resistance and hatred André had erected. Unless she could finally gain his trust. And if not—

"I never meant for you to find out this way," she said at last, to fill the awful silence that roared in the room.

He let out a course bark of laughter. "Forgive me for not believing you."

The thought of being unable to bridge this impasse made her queasy. "I'm going to my room."

André cut her a sharp glare and cringed at the dark smudges beneath her eyes. She looked ready to collapse.

Guilt niggled at him, for he was responsible for her long, arduous journey here. He'd gone to Las Vegas to kidnap a scheming mistress, not an expectant mother. What the hell had he brought on himself?

Time would tell. For now he'd err on the side of caution. "Come. I'll escort you to your room."

She glared at him. "So you can lock me in again?"

He affected a negligent shrug as he longed to throw something—ah, she *did* speak to his inner beast. He waited until she'd started up the stairs before following her up.

"My apology for doing so earlier." His fit of anger had been so reminiscent of his father that he still longed to rail at himself.

"But you did it anyway," she said.

"You have my word that it won't happen again."

"Your word?" She laughed, a glacial sound vibrating with anger. "Why would I believe you?"

He grabbed her arm and tugged her to him, wanting to see her face when he replied. "Because, unlike your previous protector, I stand by my promises."

She jerked free, her arms banding her middle to hug her tiny waist as he longed to do, amber eyes condemning him. "Tell me, André. Did you vow fidelity to your fiancée?"

"No."

Clearly his admission was the last thing she'd expected, for the flush of anger left her cheeks, leaving her exhaustion plain to see. He huffed out an annoyed breath at himself. Continuing this war of words served no purpose tonight.

"Seek your bed, *ma chérie*."

She stared at him, as if trying to see into his heart, his soul. A waste, for the lock to both was rusted shut and the key lost to painful experience.

"I don't understand you, André," she said.

"There is no reason why you should."

André turned and sought his own room, leaving her to think what she would of him. It mattered little to him that she didn't understand his motives.

Anger boiled in him—at himself, for he'd believed her when she'd admitted she was *enceinte*. He'd taken her at her word, which showed how dangerous she was to him.

He needed more than an admission. He needed proof.

Even then he wouldn't tie himself to a woman who stirred such fiery passion in him. A woman who'd deceived him.

Just because she might be the mother of his child, it didn't mean he had to include her in his life. If the child proved to be his, he could easily gain custody of his heir and banish Kira Montgomery from their lives.

She was a schemer. A puppet of Bellamy's who'd thought nothing of doing the unthinkable. She didn't deserve to be in charge of an innocent life.

Kira had smoothly lied to him from the start. He had proof. Proof didn't lie, didn't deceive.

She bore watching closely, for her will was strong. So were her wiles, and she knew how to use them to get her way. While her *femme fatale* act had won Bellamy over, it wouldn't work on him.

But it had—and that shamed him.

He should not find her desirable—shouldn't want her for his own. But he craved her with a hunger that startled him.

His body burned with need, even knowing what he did about her, knowing she would betray him the first chance she got. He loathed the crippling emotion and refused to be ruled by it.

As he'd watched Kira gain control of her emotions earlier, he'd realized she hated the attraction she had for him as well. She pulled him to her, a powerful, sensual magnet that he struggled to resist.

Oui, André was not alone in his passion. She wanted him with a fierceness that rivaled his. She would have given herself to him in the pool if he'd pushed. He'd come close to doing just that!

She was his for the taking. He knew it, and she did as well. He could have had her tonight if he chose to, but she'd expected that. Planned it! The damn paparazzi had even circled his waters like sharks!

Though he believed she was with child, he knew better than to trust a woman—especially one who'd deceived him before. Was still deceiving him.

He'd buy a pregnancy test kit in Martinique tomorrow and verify her condition. And after that?

After that, they'd wait to learn the baby's paternity.

And while they waited she'd be his willing mistress, for there'd be no reason to deny what they both wanted.

Kira woke well past the first blush of dawn, stretching in the downy bed like a sated cat. She couldn't recall when she'd felt so rested. Sleep had been a stranger to her of late—she'd endured weeks of minimal rest even before her arduous journey to Petit St. Marc.

She sighed, lulled by the distant crash of the sea to the shore and the foreign caw and trill of exotic birds. Most were distant or muffled, but all were soothing. She could lie in bed for hours—something she rarely did.

The creak of the rattan chair in her room seemed overly loud. Her nerves tightened, the calming mood gone.

She wasn't alone.

Kira gathered the sheet to her chin and stared toward the chair. Her pulse quickened when her gaze lit on André's tall form lounging negligently across from the bed, watching her.

"Bonjour," he said, rising with fluid grace to cross to the bed with lazy purpose.

The closer he got, the clearer she read the impatience in his dark eyes. What now?

"Good morning," she replied, and hoped it would be.

He sat a box on the bedside table. "I have it on good authority that these tests are reliable."

Her gaze flicked from his to the box, then back to him. "You want me to take a pregnancy test?"

"Oui. It is suggested one should take it first thing."

A fact she knew well, since she'd gone through this procedure when her cycle had been uncharacteristically late. Her doctor had confirmed the test was right—she was pregnant.

Yet André demanded proof again.

She shrugged, hiding her annoyance that he distrusted her so. "As soon as you leave I'll take it, and satisfy your curiosity."

"I'll wait."

He had to be kidding. But one look at the firm set to his mouth confirmed he was dead serious.

"Fine. Just give me a moment." She left the bed and padded to the *en suite* bathroom. "Alone," she added, when she sensed him following her.

She took the test, as prescribed, then carried the stick out into the room. "It takes five minutes."

He checked his watch and nodded, his features a stony mask of indifference. An odd tension hummed between them to keep her on edge. What went through his mind? And, more importantly, could he love their baby?

Thirty seconds before time was up, he strode to her side and stared down at the test she held. As if it had awaited his arrival, a pink line materialized in the window.

"It is positive," he said. "You are *enceinte*."

She shook her head as she disposed of the test stick, her smile rueful. "I admitted that."

He stared at her for a long, uncomfortable moment, as if expecting her to say more. And she wanted to talk to him, for she had no idea how he felt about having a child.

"But who is the father?" he asked.

"I've told you already."

"*Oui*, once."

"Once is enough." He could either believe her, or wait six months for the test that would prove she'd told him the truth.

"You surprise me, *ma chérie*. I expected you would *insist* that the baby you carry is mine and not Bellamy's," he said, his eyes dark and accusatory.

"Why should I bother? You don't believe a word I say."

"For once we are in agreement." He strode to the door, back straight and broad shoulders stiff. "You will remain my guest until you have the baby."

"Your prisoner, you mean," she said.

"If you choose to look at it that way."

"Fine—play the tyrant," she said, so angry she could scream. But he'd expect that, and she'd not surrender to hysterics. Not now. "I can work on my laptop from here as easily as I can from the Chateau."

He stopped at the door, his expression incredulous. At last she'd gotten some reaction from him. But in a flash it was gone, replaced by the hard look she'd come to hate.

"Your only job until you give birth is to take care of yourself and the baby," he said.

"I can do that and continue working."

"Out of the question."

"Why? Have you fired me?"

"You have a new job now," he said, leaving her to wonder. "Or have you so quickly forgotten your condition?"

She glared at him, chafing at the order. "Not likely. I'll be pregnant for another six months. If I don't have something with which to occupy my time I'll go out of my mind."

His smile came slowly—a thief of passion, sneaking in unaware. The sensual curl to his mouth sent heat unfurling in her and reminded her just how much she craved his touch, his kiss. Just how responsive she was to him.

"I will endeavor to keep you busy, *ma chérie*." And with that he was gone.

Kira pressed her fists to her temples, so frustrated with André's high-handedness she could scream. If she stayed she'd become his mistress. But no matter how appealing it would be to lose herself in his arms again, to stay placed her in a dangerous game she feared she'd not win.

For once André discovered she was a Bellamy, he'd treat her with the same hatred he harbored for Edouard and Peter. He'd hate her *and* their child.

She had to contact her solicitor today. She had to find out who had set her up to look like Peter's accomplice.

Perhaps when the truth was out in the open she and André could reach a rational decision regarding the future of the Chateau and their child? And their own relationship? She could only hope.

Kira paced her room, wondering how she'd manage to sneak into André's office and ring up her solicitor. It would have to be when he left the house. Even then she'd have to be careful, for Otillie was always around.

Kira dressed quickly in khaki capri pants and a floral blouse that made her eyes gleam like rich amber and enriched the auburn highlights in her hair.

She slipped into comfortable espadrilles and made her way downstairs to the dining room. Otillie appeared almost immediately, which confirmed what Kira feared—the housekeeper was watching her closely.

She took a seat and forced a casual mien. "Will André be joining me for breakfast?"

"No," Otillie said, as she set an assortment of thinly sliced baguettes topped with ruby-tinted jelly and chocolate-filled croissants on the table. "Monsieur Gauthier ate earlier."

"Perhaps I'll see him at lunch, then."

Otillie frowned as she poured coffee that smelled rich and strong. "*Monsieur* will not return until this afternoon. He requested dinner at seven, and will join you then, *oui?*"

"Of course. I'll enjoy the beach, then," she said, hoping Otillie would take her at her word.

The older woman looked her up and down, then nodded. "*Bonjour, mademoiselle.*"

Kira ate a croissant, though her appetite was nil, then left the table. She resisted the urge to rush into André's office, and waited until Otillie disappeared into the kitchen.

Her nerves twanged a discordant beat as she slipped into his masculine domain. She hadn't been in this room in three months, yet it looked the same. With one exception. There was no telephone evident.

She searched everywhere, her frustration rising. He must have anticipated she'd try to place a call and removed the phone. He'd trumped her plan. Or so he thought.

Kira was not to be deterred—not on something as important as discovering who was set on discrediting her. She knew none of the cottages had telephones, yet there must be one at the restaurant.

Fifteen minutes later she slipped into the only restaurant on the island. A guard sat at the bar, which was manned by a tall thin Carib.

"*Bonjour, mademoiselle,*" the bartender said. "What is your pleasure?"

"Sparkling water with a twist of lime," she said as she claimed a stool at the end of the bar.

From here she had a good view of behind the bar. But the

only telephone visible was the mobile hooked to the bartender's belt.

Feeling defeated, Kira grabbed her glass of water and took a stroll along the beach. She saw more guards positioned at the dock. Though they appeared to be resting, she knew they were watching her.

Kira continued onward, down the leeward side of the island away from the public beach, so frustrated she wanted to scream.

Petit St. Marc was a beautiful prison, a verdant green rainforest surrounded by white sand. The turquoise sea rolled in an endless expanse toward the horizon, broken only by a passing ship that was soon out of sight. She walked around the spit of land that jutted into the froth of water and stepped into a protected cay.

She caught a glimpse of a guard patrolling the beach before he disappeared around an outcropping. Closer to her, a Carib boy stood on the crescent of sand, staring out to sea. Kira followed his gaze.

Not far offshore she spotted a sleek kayak, slicing through the water with apparent ease. And far out in the water she spied the unmistakable green of trees. Another island?

Of course. The kayak must have come from there.

A daring plan teased her mind as she stood in the protection of the rocks while the mariner rowed toward the shore. Just before the lime-green kayak reached the beach the young Carib bounded out and pulled the shallow boat the rest of the way onto the sand.

The two boys ran up the track and disappeared into the forest. Her gaze flitted from the kayak to the other island. There'd be a telephone there—one that was not guarded.

If she left immediately she could ring her solicitor and be back on the island before anyone missed her. She'd know what Claude had found out in her absence. But she'd have to journey there in the kayak first.

Her stomach knotted at the thought of riding such a distance in a small watercraft. Her terror of small boats tended to paralyze her with fear. But this was her best chance to speak at length with her solicitor.

With Claude's aid she could get to the bottom of this deception. But first she had to overcome her phobia.

She closed her eyes, trembling from head to toe, her stomach tossing like a storm-tossed sea. Dark memories of the boating accident darted from their shadows to taunt her. The pitch of the boat on Lake Mead. Her mother's squeal of laughter as her newest lover drove the speedboat at a reckless speed. The sharp turn that had pitched Kira from the boat. The suffocating water that had rushed over her head, the numbing cold, the blackness that had seemed eternal.

Kira opened her eyes on a gasp, the wedge of green lying before her a blur through her tears. She couldn't do it. Her fear was too great.

Yet even as she admitted it she knew she had to try.

Kira darted an uncertain glance at the forest. The boys had yet to return. Nobody else was around. This was her chance to slip away. Now.

Her stomach quivered and her knees trembled as she inched toward the kayak. One step. Two.

She had to think of her child. Of convincing André she wasn't the conniving tart he believed her to be. This was the only way.

Yet even as she maneuvered the light vessel around and jumped in, she wondered if she could trust her solicitor with this request.

What if he was the one who'd set her up for this fall? Kira wondered as she put to sea. Who could she trust? Nobody.

André, her heart whispered.

No! It was too soon to trust him. She concentrated on rowing the kayak.

The first swell propelled the craft high on a wave and dropped it. Terror coursed through her in electrifying ripples. Her hands tightened so on the rounded handle of the paddle, fighting the waves that threatened to force her back to Petit St. Marc.

A young boy had managed it. Surely she could as well?

Kira focused on making the paddle work for her instead of against her. But reading about kayaking and doing it were two different things, further complicated by her numbing fear of sitting so low on the sea.

The salt spray stung her skin. The strong lap of the waves against the fiberglass kayak kept her on edge.

She dipped the paddle in the turquoise brine and thought of the men in her life. The promises made. Broken. The love she'd hoped to find that remained elusive.

The soul-searing passion she'd shared with just one man. André. The precious baby they'd created.

The past month she'd thought of coming back to him. Having lived her life embroiled in secrets, she'd grown to despise them. And now that he'd brought her back she was cloaked in more secrets that could destroy their future.

She kept her gaze trained on the island ahead. It still seemed small and remote. How long would it take to get there?

Hopefully not long. She needed to be back on Petit St. Marc when André returned.

Kira longed to give her weary arms a rest from rowing, but the sudden change in the wind was whipping her off course. It took all her strength to keep the kayak headed toward her destination.

She glanced back at Petit St. Marc. Though she was far from the island, it still loomed large and mysterious, much like its owner.

Her stomach rolled like the sea, growing angrier by the second. So did the wall of clouds hunkering on the horizon, stretching high and ominous in a blue sky that was quickly growing black.

A storm was approaching fast. Being out on the water in the small kayak doused her in renewed fear.

She'd made a mistake setting to sea. The clouds boiled into a tower that looked more ominous than André's temper. She'd never make it to shore before the squall broke.

As if in agreement, a gust of wind hit her, lifting the kayak and sending it shooting a good ten feet in the wrong direction. Panic squeezed a scream from her. She shook so badly her knees knocked against the fiberglass hull of the craft.

The swell crashed over her, drenching her to the skin. Then again as it tossed the kayak further off course.

Kira forced her weary arms to work the paddle, slicing in the choppy water. Again and again. Fighting against the storm and her choking panic, knowing if she gave up she would die.

She was close enough to see details of the island's shore-line. Her heart sank and new fear exploded within her.

The island was minuscule compared to Petit St. Marc—a heavily wooded dome that crashed into the sea, leaving a shore-line littered with treacherous rocks.

Her arms shook so badly with fear and exhaustion she could barely row. But she couldn't stop. She couldn't put ashore here.

It was too dangerous. She had to push on.

Surely she'd find a village on the other side?

Lightning streaked overhead and she jumped, nearly dropping the paddle. Her heart pounded so hard she grew light-headed.

Kira tried to skirt the side of the island. Her arms ached, her shoulders burned, and her stomach lurched with dread. But it was her mind that taunted her the most, chiding her for making a mistake that could kill herself and her child.

The sky opened. Rain pelted her, blinded her. Her clothes molded to her. Her long hair was plastered to her face and back. Water filled the small kayak.

Still she fought the paddle, fought the swell of the waves, fought her panic. She couldn't stop, couldn't rest until she got past the last cluster of jagged rocks that had turned black and sinister in the deluge.

The whine of a high-powered engine sliced through the rumble of a storm. Someone else was out in this weather. Coming closer. Perhaps the Carib boy's father? Perhaps someone who could help her?

She whimpered with exhaustion and darted past the last out-cropping, knowing to stop would send the kayak crashing into the rocks. But her strength was deserting her.

The engine's whine grew closer. Closer. Apprehension skipped down her spine.

Nobody should be out in this weather. Yet she was, and she wasn't alone.

She risked a quick glance back, hoping to see who was there, catching a glimpse of a man riding the crest of a wave.

André? No!

How had he found her so quickly?

It didn't matter. He was here. She had absolute trust he'd save her, if only to upbraid her for setting to sea in a storm.

As if mocking her attempt to stay alive, a gust of wind broadsided the kayak. The paddle was ripped from her hands. The wind stole her scream. In a blink, the kayak flipped over.

Sea water was shoved into her face and enveloped her, dragging her down. Down. Down.

Dark.

Suffocating.

And her nightmare came back to life.

André's heart stopped, only to start with a vengeance and race with the fury of the wind. He'd kill her for doing something so foolish, for putting herself and his baby in harm's way.

But first he had to rescue her and see them safely onto Noir Creux. First he had to play the part of a fool again.

He cut the Jet Ski's engine and dove into the spot where he'd seen her go down. He ticked off minutes in his mind, knowing time was precious. Crucial.

He died by centimeters as he searched the murky depths churned by the storm and didn't find her. He stretched out, swimming fast and hard, pushing through the black water until his lungs burned.

Finally his fingers grazed skeins of silk. He wound a hand

in the thick mass of hair and reeled her to him, then anchored her close and pushed them both to the surface at the same time.

Her fingers digging into his arms gave him hope, energy, profound relief. His choking fear died, only to give birth to an anger that made the storm pale in comparison.

They broke the surface together, pounded by rain and battered by waves, limbs entwined, gazes locked on one another. He read the fear and need and relief in her eyes. He recoiled from the odd tangled emotions that sank into him.

He didn't want to feel more for her than lust. All he wanted was to capture her desire. But she took more. More than he had to offer. More than he wanted to give.

After his jaunt to Martinique to meet with his solicitor he knew why. For her impassioned vow that the Chateau was her home was a lie. She was an opportunist, flitting from one benefactor to another.

But not with him. He had the upper hand now, and he didn't intend to relinquish it.

It was just as well she didn't understand the turmoil eddying within him. She was an enchantress who wouldn't hesitate to use his weakness toward her to further her goal.

He wrapped an arm around her tiny waist and struck out for shore, aware of the pitfalls he'd memorized years before. The press of her body against his was sheer torture.

Before his private hell had enveloped his life she'd been the type of woman he'd desired. Not just as a lover. No, as his mate.

But that had been an eternity ago.

He wasn't the same man he'd been back then.

He'd lost patience with the gentler side that demanded trust, fidelity. Love.

He couldn't give any woman those things. All he could offer was his protection. Money. Unbridled passion.

André certainly would never offer even that to his enemy, no matter how much he desired her. No matter that she likely carried his heir.

After an eternity, André felt the black grit of volcanic sand beneath him. He pushed from the surf, dragging her with him, her fingernails digging into his arm attesting to her fear.

She was his for the taking. One word, one touch, and she'd tumble into his arms.

That would be too easy, stripping him of any satisfaction of conquering her. Of catching her at her own duplicity.

The rain battered them now, as merciless as his feelings toward her. He trudged through the churning surf between towering rocks slicked by rain, her by his side, her essence coursing through his blood, luring him in.

A black hole loomed ahead and he ran into it, pulling her in beside him. Only then did he draw a decent breath. Only then did he look at her. Only then did he realize his heart was close to beating out of his chest.

Fury. That was why. Any other reason was unacceptable.

The deep shadows in the cave obscured her features. So he focused on each indrawn breath, each stutter of sound, each ripple of sensation that sped from her hand into his.

"Do you feel all right?" he dared to ask.

"Yes. Fine." He heard her swallow, felt another tremor go from her, and he cursed the span of concern he felt for her. "We are all right."

She and the baby were alive. He was alive. And they were marooned together until the storm abated.

He detested the fact she'd ensnared him in such seclusion. Even though he knew what he knew about her, she made him feel things that made no sense to him, that he'd never experienced before. That scared the hell out of him.

Yet he ached to make her his right now. Again. Alone in this primitive cave while the storm raged outside and his own tempest battered within him, when nothing and nobody could interrupt them this time.

He wanted to pound into her with the same intensity as the

storm pummeled the islet. He wanted to break down her defenses and for once hear her admit the truth.

Mon Dieu! She'd drive him mad with her stubborn nature and siren's body. She was a contradiction that defied reason.

How could she be terrified of small boats, yet risk her life in one today? To escape him. That was why.

She'd have done anything to flee the trap she'd ended up in, for a fortune awaited her. Yet how could she have known?

Damn her! "Have you no regard for my child?"

He felt her stiffen, sensed her muscles bunching as if to pull away from him. "I—I only meant to find a telephone here, then return to Petit St. Marc."

No doubt she'd been desperate to contact Peter and confirm if the deal had gone through. If so, she'd have found a way to disappear. Her error in seeking help here, coupled with the storm, had thwarted that plan. It had dumped her right back into André's lap. Just where he wanted her.

"You would've waited an eternity. Noir Creux is uninhabited. A nature sanctuary under the protection of France." He hauled her against his side, stopping her retreat. "And me."

"You watch over a nature sanctuary?" Incredulity rang in her voice.

"I watch over many precious things." Like her?

The thought came unbidden and was met with immediate resistance. She was more dangerous than a hurricane. Her carnal sting more lethal than a scorpion's.

"Noir Creux is unique," he said at last, when his pulse had ceased hammering in his veins, when his need to take her had abated. "An extinct volcanic dome is attached to a coral reef. Both are ancient."

"Any buried treasure?"

"Oui," he said, attuned to her every word, to every subtle shift of her body, to the wild scent of the storm mingling with warm woman. "But to attempt to remove it would destroy something far more valuable than doubloons."

"You surprise me, André." The comment was soft. Intimate, yet tinged with awe.

His fingers curled into fists. He didn't want her admiration, her praise. He didn't want to think that she'd be more than willing to tumble into his arms now that he'd proved he cared about something other than making millions. Or was it just another act?

It didn't matter anymore. He wanted her.

Here.

Fast.

Hard.

Kira was his booty, fetched from the sea. His prize to savor. His to command. Yet the life within her tempered him like nothing else had. Life they'd likely created.

She'd gotten to him, breached his defenses, made him deal with emotions he'd vowed never to feel. He hated the doubts that crept into his mind. Hated second-guessing himself. Hated that she had lied to him from the start.

It would stop now.

He wouldn't be swayed by her excuses.

He had to throw up walls again.

He had to gain the upper hand.

He had just the means to make her hate him.

"You could have asked more for your shares, *ma chérie*," he said.

"Shares?"

"*Oui*. Your stock in the Chateau."

He heard her breath catch, felt tension eddy from her in icy waves. "I didn't put a price on my shares because they aren't for sale."

Mon Dieu, was all that came from her mouth lies? "I received a call early this morning, giving me first chance to buy your shares. Just like Edouard's were offered to me."

"This can't be happening," she said. "Who called you?"

"It doesn't matter."

"Yes, it does, because I won't sell."

"You can't change your mind now."

"I most certainly can. I never approved a sale. My God, I have to call my solicitor, stop this before—"

"It's too late. I paid your price," he said. "As of an hour ago, Chateau Mystique is one hundred percent mine."

CHAPTER SIX

KIRA moved toward the mouth of the cave, her feet leaden, feeling cold and hollow inside. She'd thought she'd survived the worst life could fling at her. How naïve she'd been.

When Edouard had promoted her from hospitality manager of his elite Le Cygne Hotel in London to significant minority stockholder of Chateau Mystique, she'd been terrified and anxious. She'd wanted to please Edouard. Wanted to prove to him that she could run a luxury hotel, that she was worthy of his attention at last.

But she'd barely settled in when tragedy had struck. A car accident had taken the life of Edouard's mistress and left him in critical condition.

That was when André Gauthier had struck, offering an out-rageous sum for the whole of the Chateau. Edouard, through his solicitor Claude, had delivered a firm no—the Chateau wasn't for sale. But André had persisted, and Kira had feared for Edouard's recovery in the face of so much turmoil.

She'd said as much to Claude, who'd quickly arranged that meeting between Kira and André on Petit St. Marc. A meeting André still swore he'd known nothing about.

That was when she'd engaged in the most bracing debate of her life. That was when she'd lost a bit of her heart to André Gauthier.

Not once had she surrendered her stance on the availability of the Chateau, but she'd caved to his sensual demands.

The day after she'd returned to Las Vegas Edouard had died. Kira had mourned him in her own way, for though he'd been her father, she'd barely known him.

He'd made it clear when she was very young that he would provide for her, but he'd never give her his name. He would keep her apart from his legitimate family—the two would never become one. She was never to admit her paternity to anyone, and if she did he'd disinherit her.

She'd done as he'd asked because she'd been a child and alone. Because she'd known no better.

He had educated her and given her a job at his London hotel, but the biggest surprise had come when he'd brought her to America and given her shares in the Chateau. He'd made it clear that this was all she'd get from him, and his own shares wouldn't pass to her until his death.

It had been enough. She'd had great plans to improve the hotel on the Vegas strip, and she'd had a chance to finally know her father.

But tragedy had struck first. And now, through an act of deceit, André owned it all.

And she had nothing but false promises.

She stared out at the rain sheeting over the islet. Had the person who'd trumped up documents to make it appear as if she'd conspired with Peter Bellamy to ruin André also forged her name to dispose of her shares? Had they done the same with Edouard's shares as well?

Who had that much corporate power? Peter Bellamy?

According to Edouard, when Peter had discovered Kira's existence his legitimate son had resented her. Had her half-brother sought to ruin her? If so, he'd done a good job of it, for both acquisitions had gotten past Claude, her and Edouard's solicitor.

It could take years of litigation to regain her shares. She had no money. No resources. Nothing but a baby growing in her. While André had wealth and control on his side.

How utterly foolish she'd been to think she could come to terms with him. "How much did you pay?" she asked.

"You know the answer."

"How much?" she asked, her voice cracking.

His pause stretched an eternity. "Two million."

A fortune. *Her* fortune.

Kira pressed her head against the damp stone wall of the cave, feeling dry and burned up inside. Used and tossed aside like refuse.

She doubted the funds had gone into her account. No, whoever had plotted this embezzlement would have escaped with it.

Kira pressed a palm over the cold stone, so chilled by her bleak future that she barely felt the dampness seep deeper into her. She didn't know what to do now. Didn't know what she could possibly do.

She stared at the rain coursing over the rocks, each droplet knowing its destination. Gravity guided it, though the water was happy to stay its course, to rush on and join a larger pool, its identity lost in the community of water, joining the mass for the common good of the sea.

Kira envied those droplets, for as of now she had nowhere to go. No one to turn to for help. No family waiting to take her in. No purpose. Nothing.

All because of a traitor at the Chateau and André Gauthier's thirst for vengeance.

She'd known André was ruthless, that he was a corporate raider who attained whatever he set out to conquer. He'd never lied about wanting the Chateau.

But she hadn't guessed he'd be so relentless in his pursuit of it. That he'd abduct her in his quest for vengeance, then cut her out of her inheritance without remorse. That it would be so easy for him to achieve his goal with the destruction of her own.

Her own naïveté was much to blame, for she'd believed the

trouble she'd faced at the Chateau had stemmed from a few disloyal employees who'd resented her sudden elevated status. She'd never dreamed someone was plotting her ruin.

Or were they? Could she truly believe André? Had *he* paid the traitor to do this bit of nasty business?

Her heart said no, that he'd simply been waiting for the opportunity to present itself. But her heart was too hungry for love to be trusted. Her heart was too open, too innocent—easy bait for the sly and cunning of the species. Like André?

He had the power to engineer such a takeover. The ruthless bent to take what he wanted by any means.

"Who is the conspirator?" she asked, too heartsick to cry or raise her voice. "I have a right to know his name."

"How would I know?"

She whirled on him, blinking once, then again, before she saw him in the gloom. The shadows fit him well.

"Don't lie to me," she said. "You must have paid someone at the Chateau to do your bidding. Someone who would forge my name on documents so nobody would question why my stocks were offered to you, making your takeover complete."

"I don't resort to underhanded dealings."

She jerked her chin up, willing him to read the movement as defiant. Livid. "Just kidnapping?"

"Don't bait me, *ma chérie*."

"Why not?" She moved toward him, trembling with anger as well as anxiety, tired of his bullying. "You stripped me of my home and my job. My dream. I have nothing left to lose."

"No?"

He flung an arm around her and jerked her to him. Her breasts flattened against his chest, her stomach rubbing his taut belly. His powerful arms banded hers to her sides.

His captive. His desire. His!

She felt his dominance in every breath he took. Felt his savage need course from him into her, fueling her own wants which she could barely contain.

Kira knew the folly in trying to break free, so she stood as stiff as a statue and braced herself for a kiss meant to dominate. To punish.

Let him take. She could give no more.

For surely an arrogant man like André, who was this close to the edge, would take her now? He'd be driven to punish her for challenging him. He wouldn't be satisfied until he controlled everything about her.

Like the last time they'd ended up entwined in each other's arms? Making love with a fever that had threatened to consume them? That had created a life?

His head bent to hers, slowly, his gaze afire with need and something else she couldn't recognize. She trembled, wanting him so badly she shook.

But she had to be strong—for her child. For her self-respect. That was all she had left. Kira turned her head, denying him.

Instead of his expected spate of anger, one strong, masculine hand slipped between their bodies and splayed on her belly. Tremors coursed through her with terrifying force, mocking her with a sense of rightness she was loath to admit. Firing her blood and her anger in turn.

But it was her heart that paused, warmed, softened. For surely that protective palm, pressed where their child thrived, meant he cared?

"I will file for complete custody," he said, his lips grazing the tender skin behind her ear. But instead of heat, she felt chilled to the bone.

He couldn't be that cold. That heartless. Yet he wasn't a man to make idle threats either.

"You can't mean that," she said.

"But I do, *ma chérie*. The baby binds us together now, but after the birthing that will change."

The forewarning speared her heart and soul, honing her maternal instincts to protect her baby however she must. How could she have thought she had nothing more to lose? That she had a chance for a future with André?

She'd do anything to keep her child. Anything.

She would not lose this battle.

Kira turned her head, her gaze seeking his in the minimal light. His resolute features confirmed he knew her weakness as well. And he knew how to use that against her.

Certainly whoever had sculpted his beautiful mouth had seduction in mind. She felt her own lips tingle, remembering the firmness of his mouth molded to hers, the provocative bow that tickled and teased and tempted her to shed her inhibitions. She had only to shift a little and lift her face to his to steal a kiss, to take the initiative again. She wouldn't. She couldn't. But, oh, how she longed to!

And his eyes—my God, she could drown in their mesmerizing depths.

"You can't seriously mean to take my child from me." Because it was wrong and cruel. Because it would kill her to be cut from her child's life.

"It is for the best," he said, his voice lethally low and as impassive as his gaze. "I am wealthy and can provide for my heir."

"I'll fight you."

"You will lose."

She didn't doubt that he was right, that he'd pull strings to get his way. But she wouldn't capitulate either. Not on this. Not ever.

"Then I'll seek joint custody—"

"No. After this reckless stunt you pulled today, you can't be trusted to care for my baby."

Unbidden tears stung her eyes and she looked away, feeling frantic now, refusing to give him the satisfaction of knowing he'd brought her low again. She gathered her courage around her, ready to plead with him to have a heart, then reminded herself he had none. For no man possessing compassion would attempt to rip a child from his mother's arms.

"I'll fight you until my very last breath," she said again, her fingers bunching his wet shirtfront. "I'll never willingly give up my child."

A charged silence rebounded off the cave walls, the tension punctuated by the rain that had reduced to a gentle patter, as if hushing to hear what he'd say. But time crawled by and he didn't respond. Didn't so much as move a muscle.

Slowly, sunlight crept into the cave, as if the heavens were rolling up their blinds. Even the air had become heavy and still, as if holding its breath in anticipation of his reply.

"Nor will I," he said at last, his arms tightening a fraction in a parody of a hug before releasing her.

Kira stepped away from him, knowing things would only get worse when the truth came out, certain that whatever bargain she struck with André must be done soon. "I'll never accept being a passing moment in my baby's life."

Some emotion flickered in his eyes—something beyond hate or lust or cold calculation. Something that gave her a thin thread of hope. She grabbed onto to it and held tight.

She trusted that André would never be so cruel as to rip her baby from her arms, from her heart. But if she was wrong…

André ran a hand over his hair, slicking the wet strands back off his tanned brow, his features unreadable as he motioned to the cave entrance. "It's time we returned to Petit St. Marc."

"How?"

She doubted she had the strength to paddle the kayak back to the island, even if she could find it. Most likely the small craft was lost to the sea.

"With luck, my Jet Ski rode out the squall."

"And if it didn't?" she asked.

He lifted one broad shoulder in a negligent shrug and left the cave. She took a deep breath, stretching her hands forward and then tightening her fingers into fists. Once. Twice.

But it did no good. Her hands still trembled, her stomach still pitched, and her heart still ached with old worries and new. For if she couldn't reach his heart, she'd have to escape the island before her baby was born. She'd have to disappear. Start over. Hide the rest of her life. For a man like André would never let her best him.

Kira quit the cave and stepped onto the rain-soaked black sand beach. As she'd expected, there was no sign of the kayak.

Its burial at sea was fitting, since a pirate had seized control of her hotel. Her life. Her future.

Out with the old.

In with the new.

Her gaze flitted to André, knee-deep in the frothy surf, inspecting a long, sleek Jet Ski. His hair glistened blue-black in the now blinding sun, the thick mass waving in artful precision over the strong column of his neck.

He'd removed his shirt to reveal a bronzed back beautifully chiseled with muscles that bunched and bulged with each movement. She remembered the feel of that power beneath her fingers as she ran her hands up and down his back, clinging to him, scoring his flesh as he took her beyond any passion that she'd known. The firm smooth texture of his skin beneath her palms. The hint of salt on her tongue that had made her thirsty for more of him.

Her fingers flexed, her body quickening as her gaze flicked over him and she remembered more. His jeans rode low on his lean waist, yet his limbs still looked long and graceful.

Once with him had not been enough.

It never would be, she admitted.

That traitorous ache of want pulsed between her legs, radiating upward to turn her limbs languid, her blood thick and hot. It scared her to be that receptive to any man. That dependent. For it allowed him to dominate her thoughts and keep her on edge.

Just like she'd been all her life. The cycle had to end.

She was so tired of being dominated by powerful men. So weary of having no say in anything.

Oh, Edouard had given her *carte blanche* for implementation of new services at the Chateau. But the long hours she'd pored over the plans had been for naught.

The Chateau was lost to her. It was just another cherished dream that had failed. All because André had chosen to exert his iron control over her.

But he was wrong about one thing. Taking her child from her wasn't for the best. She'd prove it to him. And if his heart still remained hardened, she'd simply disappear.

Talk was nonexistent on the trip back to Petit St. Marc. Not only did the whine of the Jet Ski make conversation nearly impossible, André suspected Kira was too engrossed battling her fear of an even smaller faster sea vessel.

André knew her fingernails would leave marks on his belly. She clung to him, pressing her face to his back, as if branding herself to him there as well.

Her terror rippled through her, tempering his speed as surely as the heat of her passion had burned him earlier. He felt her in every fiber of his being, each indrawn breath, each telling beat of his heart.

He wanted to hate her. Did hate her for siding with Peter Bellamy against him. Yet he desired her with an intensity he'd never felt before.

The admission worried him, for it had been that way from the beginning. When she'd first walked into his study on Petit St. Marc he'd been gripped with lust. He'd had to have her.

Even now, knowing she was in league with his enemy did not lessen his desire. He had the proof of her role in this charade tucked away in his safe, yet he wanted Kira Montgomery in his bed. Wanted his name on her lips when he brought her to climax.

And then what?

The question nagged at him as he killed the engine and beached the Jet Ski. He climbed off and helped her alight, reluctant to release her hand. So he didn't.

For once she wasn't pulling away from him either.

That glint of determination he noted in her eyes intrigued him. Now that they were on firm land, he imagined her mind was busy thinking of ways to convince him she needed to remain an integral part of her child's life.

She didn't need to bother.

He already knew she'd be a good mother.

The thought had embedded itself in André when she stood up to him, fire in her eyes, chin lifted proud, despite the telling tremors that streaked through her. He'd experienced a moment's shame for tossing out the barbarous threat that he'd bar her from their child's life.

But how could he endure her closeness either? Dare to trust her knowing that she'd repeatedly lied to him?

He didn't know. The fact he was not ready to leave her company when he had things to do in his office annoyed him, but it was the truth nonetheless.

"Monsieur Gauthier!"

André looked up at the young boy running pell-mell toward him, one brown hand raised high and waving a snow-white envelope. The mail must have arrived, and Georges had determined this missive demanded his immediate attention.

He allowed a fleeting smile. The boy was eager to earn another euro for hand-delivering his mail. André knew the boy would use the money to help support his ill mother and younger siblings.

"Pour vous, monsieur," Georges said, thrusting the envelope at him with a toothy smile.

The missive was from his detective, sent to the island by courier. It must be the final report on Kira Montgomery.

Unwilling to trek to the house to reward the boy, he tossed him the keys to the Jet Ski. "Take it. It is yours."

George's eyes rounded. *"Merci—merci."*

André turned to Kira and motioned to the gate leading into his private beach. "Walk with me."

"You're going to let that boy borrow that dangerous thing?" she asked.

"No, he can have the Jet Ski."

"Why?"

"Because he is loyal. Because it pleases me."

She tipped her head back and stared up at him curiously. The angle was just perfect for the sun to streak highlights in her vibrant hair. The mass hung in rebellious curls, giving her that just-pleasured-by-a-man look.

He caught himself on the verge of smiling and shook his head, surprised again by the contradiction that was Kira Montgomery. She portrayed a refreshing innocence at times, like now, with a flush tinting her cheeks and her eyes wide with wonder.

It was a quality he'd never seen in a mistress before—certainly in none of the women he'd employed! Was it possible that Bellamy had been her first lover?

The thought of her lying with the old man rankled. He entwined his fingers with hers, his chest tightening with annoyance.

A woman with Kira's passion deserved a virile man who could match her in bed, who'd boldly explore the myriad ways they could pleasure each other, who knew how to give and take in bed.

A man who treasured a woman instead of beating her.

He had it on good authority that Edouard Bellamy's finesse in *amour* was lacking, that he was given to bouts of unparalleled jealousy and rage. He knew it was true, for he'd seen the bruises on the old man's former mistress.

André had listened in silent rage as Suzette had made excuses for Bellamy's inexcusable behavior. But she'd stayed with the old man because he had showered her with everything she wanted. She'd chosen Bellamy over her family. She'd loved their enemy.

Had Kira fallen into the same trap? Was she fatalistically loyal to Edouard Bellamy? Would she stab André in the back too?

"What makes you so angry?" she asked, breaking the silence.

He glanced at her and shrugged, pushing the past into the recesses of his mind where it belonged. "After your adventure to Noir Creux, I have reason to be angry, *n'est-ce pas*?"

"Perhaps. I just thought—" She shook her head, her expression pensive. "We need to talk, André."

He frowned, knowing she sought reassurance. It was beyond him to offer comfort, yet he was hesitant to crush her spirits again. Nothing could be gained by beating her down more.

His win was her loss. He'd bested her. So where was the feeling of satisfaction?

André motioned to a massive hammock strung between poles and shaded by a canopy of palm fronds. "This way. I'll join you in a moment."

She bit her lip, as if hesitating, then set off toward the shade without argument.

He watched her, noticing her wet clothes no longer clung to her like his hands longed to do. That was his most challenging problem, for though she'd lied to him, deceived him, he wanted to believe her. His desire for her had blinded him to her perfidy.

André shook his head and tore open the letter from his detective, his impatience with himself escalating. His gaze flew over the short message that ended with a cryptic "more to follow when I receive proof."

He scanned the note again, then read it slowly, absorbing every word. His body tensed as his ire blazed to life again. Could this be some mistake?

But, no, the detective was meticulous in his findings, checking and double-checking everything he uncovered. Which made this bit of news all the more troubling.

Just what the hell was going on? He stuffed the note in his pocket and headed across the sand that was bleached white under the sun's glare.

He'd known from the start Kira was doing Bellamy's bidding, having had proof of her involvement. He'd deduced that she'd now sold her shares in the Chateau so she could embark on a new life—escape his grasp out of fear of retaliation should the child be Bellamy's, or entrapment if the baby was his, as he suspected.

But the two million André had paid for complete control of the Chateau had never showed up in her account in Las Vegas or in England. Likely she'd had the money funneled into a Swiss or offshore bank account. But as soon as the thought crossed his mind he doubted its validity.

Kira hadn't had any access to a telephone—so she couldn't have made the transaction. No, the only way she could have had a hand in this sale was if she'd set it up before he took her from Las Vegas.

It was plausible, for she had admitted to ringing her solicitor, but even so she'd had no idea of his plan. Then, too, why had she refused his earlier offer to buy her shares and then turned around and given him the first crack to acquire them for the price he'd offered earlier?

It made no sense.

She wasn't a flighty businesswoman—of that he was sure. Yet this offer made it seem that way.

Everything she'd queried him about on Noir Creux came back to him. Her surprise at his acquisition and at the amount he'd paid for her shares. The anger, panic and defeat when she'd realized it was a done deal.

Her admission that she'd risked her life just to phone her solicitor to find out the truth. She wasn't lying—of that he was sure.

His mouth pulled into a grim line at that admission. Whether she was the injured party or not, there was nothing he could do about it now. If his detective turned up anything that nullified Kira he'd take action then.

André scanned the beach for Kira. He spotted her, staring forlornly out to sea.

A chill tripped up his spine when he thought how close she'd come to dying. *Mon Dieu*, he had nearly lost them both!

His woman. His child.

A strange warmth expanded in his chest as he allowed himself to believe the truth in his heart. If she was to be believed he'd soon be a father. Not Bellamy. Him—André Gauthier.

It was sobering.

He and his former fiancée had discussed having a family once. She'd wanted two—no more than that! And she hadn't wished to start a family until they'd been married at least three years. No exceptions.

He'd agreed, simply because it was a solid plan. Controlled, like every facet of his life. Because his impending marriage had been nothing more than a business deal.

Then Kira had burst into his life, vibrant and fiery as the morning sun. Her blinding light had exposed the rigidity of his life—she'd roused his anger and his lust. But her sharp mind had been the spark to ignite his interest.

Even knowing she was his enemy's plaything, he'd wanted her then.

Even knowing she'd conspired to ruin him, he still wanted her.

And, damn, he'd have her now.

André ducked under the canopy, pleased Kira was stretched out on the hammock. He kicked off his shoes and pulled his shirt over his head, letting it fall where it might. His cutoffs went next, and he heaved a relieved breath as his sex sprang free.

Her lips parted on a gasp. "What are you doing?"

"Getting comfortable." He moved toward her. The darkening glow of passion in her eyes confirmed she was battling desire without success. "Take your clothes off, *ma chérie*."

"Absolutely not! Someone could come by—"

"Not here. This is my private beach. Nobody will see you but me."

André had the satisfaction of watching her eyes widen, the pupils dilate, her breathing grow heavy. She wanted him as much as he did her, but she was clearly hesitant to shed her inhibitions or her clothes.

Contrary behavior for a mistress. But he'd come to realize Kira wasn't ordinary. *Oui*, she was a contradiction.

Sexy, yet shy.

Passionate, yet refined.

Savvy, yet reserved.

He leaned over her, noting the quickening of her breath, the flushing of her skin. His mouth grazed her soft flushed cheek, nuzzled her neck, moving slowly to where a telling pulse hammered in the slender column of her throat, keeping pace with his own wild heartbeat.

He'd never wanted a woman as much as he did her. Had never exercised such restraint in seducing a woman. But though the chase made the anticipation all the more sweeter, his patience would not last much longer.

"I've seen you naked," he said. "Why hesitate now?"

He heard her swallow, felt a shiver rip through her. "You dare to ask after you threaten to bar me from my child's life?"

He read the resolute determination in her eyes and almost smiled. Almost. She possessed more power than she realized.

"One has nothing to do with the other, *ma chérie,*" he said, his fingers releasing the tiny buttons on her blouse.

She grasped his hand, stopping him. "It has everything to do with this—this passion between us. I won't be removed from our child's life, André. Not now, not ever."

She'd thrown down the gauntlet, giving him the choice to refuse to bend, to acquiesce to her demand, or to lie. "Very well. You have my word that I won't mention it again."

"I—" She swallowed. Stared straight into his eyes. And he saw her acceptance for what it was. Trust. "Thank you."

He didn't want her gratitude. Didn't want to tie anything to this moment but mutual desire. No strings, no promises.

"Now we will make love *à la Caribbean Française, oui*?"

"Yes," she said.

Triumph surged through him, along with emotions he didn't want to face. Not now. Not when these new disturbing sensations were hammering away at him.

He pushed her blouse wide and traced a finger over the lace trim on her demi-bra, surprised his hand trembled. Stunned that with her he felt like an untried youth again.

She moaned and splayed her hands on his chest, the small

fingers flexing over his muscles. An electric jolt shot through him, his muscles snapping taut, his body quivering with need. *Mon Dieu*, but he'd never experienced such sexual awareness from a simple touch.

He stared at her, his gaze ravenous as it swept over the creamy swells of her breasts pushing above the lacy scrap of her bra. A growl of annoyance rumbled through him, for he hated the barrier. With a flick of his fingers he released the clasp.

She moaned as her bosom spilled free. He palmed a globe, intrigued by the pale silken texture of her breast against his tanned skin, of the taut puckered nipple begging for his kiss.

"You are beautiful."

The tip of her tongue flicked over the lips he longed to taste and tease. But it was her eyes, lifted to his, that sent his heart racing into overdrive. Desire, longing, trust.

"I am average," she said. "But you—you're extraordinary."

"You needn't resort to flattery to win my favor."

"I'm not," she said, her voice breathy. "It's just that I've never met a man like you before."

"Nor will you," he said, driven by a fierce possessiveness.

Raw need coursed through him, his own blood pooling hot and thick in his groin. He ached to have her. Protect her. To make her his and his alone.

The erotic drumbeat in his ears matched time with her erratic pulse as he removed the last of her clothes, until she was as naked as he. He stood there feasting on the pale curves and hollows of her body, knowing that for now she was his.

Oui, the time for waiting was over.

He'd have her here. Now. And damn the consequences.

Kira shivered with nervous energy and a good dose of shock. She'd never imagined she would enjoy lying naked beneath a man's scrutiny. And in broad daylight on a beach, no less!

But the sultry promise in André's eyes captivated her. She was under his spell, ensnared by the onslaught of his passion, a willing slave to his desire.

More than that, she trusted that he would make things right. That sometime he'd listen to her. That he'd believe she wasn't the calculating woman he'd accused her of being.

She trusted him in this. It was enough. For now.

Warmth swept over her like a welcoming summer breeze, kissing the skin he'd just bared. He was going to make love with her and she would welcome him.

She ached for him to kiss her, to touch her. But he just stood by the hammock, his gaze devouring every inch of her. And her body reacted to his scrutiny as if the touch were real, her skin pebbling and flushing, her muscles tensing, her breath growing heavy as her pulse raced out of control.

The sensations were new and intense, robbing her of will, of restraint. She couldn't push him away, not when her arms had ached to hold him to her again. Not when she'd dreamed of this moment for three long months.

Her body had throbbed in the dead of night, just remembering the wonder of his gloriously powerful form fitted to hers, moving in hers in a harmony she'd never felt before. When he'd made love to her before she'd felt their hearts beat in tandem.

She wanted that again. Had to have it.

The sensations he wrought in her defied description, but her soul knew this joining was right.

He was the flesh-and-blood man of her dreams. The father of her baby. She wanted him with a keening ache that overrode caution.

She smiled, her arms reaching for him, knowing she'd die if he didn't kiss her, touch her, love her. Knowing she must steal this moment, this memory, now, before he learned the truth.

His mouth quirked, his eyes gleaming. He rolled into the hammock, the net dipping precariously as he settled beside her.

In the perfect synchronization of the lovers' dance, her body shifted to fit against his. She focused on every nuance of the moment, skin touching skin, hard unyielding muscles pressing against soft flesh.

His hand rested on her hip, unmoving, light, yet his touch sent heat spiraling to her core. Her hand found a natural perch on his broad shoulder.

It felt right. Perfect.

It felt like forever.

But all it could ever be was now.

For the passion blazing between them would be doused the moment he learned she was Edouard Bellamy's daughter.

CHAPTER SEVEN

KIRA shifted to make more room for him, her muscles clenching deep inside her as he slid a hair-roughened thigh between hers. She trailed a hand up his muscular arm and over his shoulder, savoring the bunch of strength beneath his hot, smooth skin.

"Make love with me," she said, her hand trekking down his chest to rub a palm over his hardened nipples, feeling his body quicken.

His eyes flared with lust, his hand shifting to caress her with slow, agonizing strokes. "But of course."

Yet he made no move to hurry things along. Desperation sizzled in her. She wanted all he had to give *now*, to sink into him before she had time to analyze this driving need building and building within her. But he was clearly in no hurry.

His big hand glided down the back of her thigh and she squirmed, begging for him to touch her intimately. Instead, his hand meandered back up to her waist, and she dug her fingers into his shoulders as need rocked through her again, her body quivering like jelly.

His fingers splayed over her stomach and a different emotion gripped her, so sharp and new that it shrank her world to what mattered most: him, her and their child.

The tense expression on his face made her wonder if he felt the same. If he felt anything at all except lust and the need to maintain control.

Their child. Could he love their baby?

She closed her eyes, wishing she knew, wishing her emotions weren't so intense and raw with André, wishing what they'd shared was based on love instead of passion.

A child didn't have to be conceived in love to be loved. She would adore her baby—she already did. For once in her life, she'd have someone to love her in return.

But how would André fit into this tidy family?

Kira bit her lip, fearing he'd regard their child much like her father had treated her. She'd been a responsibility he hadn't wanted, yet he'd assumed her care at a young age and placed her in boarding school.

Strangers had raised her, praised her, nourished her as best they could. When the other students had gone home on holiday, she'd been shuffled off to a posh hotel in London and watched by a nanny. She'd never shared a birthday or Christmas with family. Never had anyone who cared about her.

That was why her child would know that he or she was loved. Her child would have a home. Security. A mother. A father?

"What is going on in that pretty head of yours?" he asked.

Us, she wanted to say, but knew that would spoil the moment. So she tucked that truth away with her other secret, that made this dream a challenge to attain.

"I was thinking how good this felt," she said, and it did.

"It gets better."

His hand swept up her ribs, leaving a trail of shivers in its wake. He palmed one breast, his thumb rubbing over the nipple until it throbbed.

She arched against him, craving his touch, craving him. Their future was as substantial as the tropical haze that hung in the dense valleys, but she ached to get lost in the sultry mist with him once more.

His head lowered a fraction. She met him halfway, their mouths brushing once, twice, before melding—a teasing glide of lips and tongues that sent a hum of need vibrating through her. She squirmed, desperate to get closer, to rub against the heat of his sex.

He obliged, grinding against her and making the hammock swing erratically. Her stomach did an odd quiver—and not a pleasant one.

She pulled back, gulping. "This might not be a good idea."

He went still, his intense eyes narrowing to convey his patience would not tolerate any of her machinations now. "You no longer wish to make love?"

She shook her head and let her own hands drift around his torso to trace the tense muscles on his back and the deep indentation of his spine. "Not here. This hammock is a rather unstable bed." And her stomach tended to get queasy.

More so since the jaunt to Noir Creux. She was also a bit light-headed, though looking up into André's magnetic eyes chased both symptoms away.

A slow smile curved his sensuous lips, and raw desire flared in his dark eyes, the combination leaving her breathless for what was to come. "But I thought you enjoyed taking risks."

"Never." Though she was taking a monstrous one now. "I'm a very proper Englishwoman. Brisk walks along well-trod paths and the like."

"How boring."

And so very lonely. But she wouldn't admit that. She'd never revealed this awful emptiness that dwelled within her to another soul. She held close the fact that with him she'd felt a connection and purpose she'd never felt before. She knew no matter how good it seemed now, their affair was tenuous at best.

"Kiss me again," she said, tangling her fingers in his hair and pulling him to her.

"With pleasure."

His mouth was sheer heaven, his kiss so deep and drugging that she couldn't think anymore. Just feel. His taste, his power, his passion were more potent than any drug.

His tongue parried with hers while his hands pillaged her body, molding her breasts, teasing the nipples until she was reeling from want. She arched against him, finding small relief as she rubbed against the hard wall of his chest like a cat in heat.

Sensations crashed within her, her heart swelling with love, her body crying for release. She was drunk on him, torturing herself with a need that the world couldn't contain.

She spread her legs wider and he settled fully against her, his engorged sex hot and hard on her belly. A whimper tore from her, for she needed him in her, filling her. She needed the connection of another soul dancing with hers.

Arching against him only intensified her frustrations, so she wrapped her legs around his hips and ground against him. She was done with the torment—done with the waiting.

His mouth left hers with a gasp, the eyes staring into hers near black. He whispered in French, his voice low, pausing to nuzzle her ear, lap at the lobe, then tug it with his teeth, sending liquid heat rushing through her.

I love him. The litany sang in her heart, filling her with wonder, chasing the dark shadows to their corners.

She moaned, grinding against him, running her hands down his back to skim the taut swell of his derrière, holding back the words that ached to break free. For she was afraid that truth would shatter the mood. Make him think. Doubt.

Her fingers dug into his taut arms as she arched against him, gasping as he shifted and his hot sex moved between her legs.

Yes, she thought, squirming, clutching his back, his ribs, his buttocks. The gentle breeze kissed her through the netting, but she burned with a sensual fever that could only be broken with completion. Only with him.

She panted with need, her senses consumed by him, her heart ensnared as well. The hammock rocked and shimmied, the ropes biting into her bare back. If he didn't make love to her soon she'd die.

His hips rocked forward, his sex pushing inside her. She gasped and smiled, clinging to him, welcoming him home, wanting more, wanting all of him.

He shifted again, pulling from her. "*Mon Dieu*, you're tight. Perfect."

She moaned, frustrated by the torture and the insatiable need for him that raged within her. He was large, powerful, and driving her mad with want.

"You are taking too long," she said, clutching at him.

He pushed into her before the last word left her mouth, filling her completely, touching her heart, her soul. The heat of his unsheathed sex sinking into her pulsing core ripped a gasp of wonder from her. She hadn't remembered this feeling from before, coming at the end of a long night of passion.

This time it felt new. A beginning. Giving birth to a hope she harbored in the secret recesses of her heart. Could it be?

The power and carnal promise in each thrust lifted her higher toward the sun, burning her with his desire, with his need. His brand of absolute possession seared her soul.

She was his. Now. Always. She accepted it. Embraced it. For she knew she'd never find this oneness with another man.

His movements came faster, deeper, keener, stealing her ability to think. He'd pushed her past reason to a shimmering aura where she could only feel, into a spray of glorious rainbows that blinded her.

She clung to him, trembling with the force of her climax, welcoming his release. Nothing she'd experienced came close to this wonderful feeling of unity.

He held her so tightly she thought they'd become one, was sure there no longer existed a place where he ended and she began.

"*Mon amour,*" he said, nearly chewing out the words.

She smiled and blinked back tears, for he'd whispered the only French she knew, the only words she'd ached to hear.

My love.

Yes, she was, she admitted, gliding her hands down his

sweat-slicked back and marveling at the steely strength rippling beneath her fingers.

She could've lain there the rest of the day, but she felt him pulling away from her. Knew this ideal had come to an end.

It was too soon. She wanted more. She wanted forever.

The hammock shimmied beneath her. She stilled and grabbed his arms, the muscles taut. He gave a swift jerk, his body bowing and pulling her flush with his.

Her breath caught in her lungs as the hammock shuddered and flipped. She yelped and clung to André.

Her world turned upside down, air whispering over her bare body, the weight of him on her removed. She sprawled on him, breast to broad chest, stomach to corded belly.

She felt his arms tremble with the strain of holding on to the hammock as he became a new cradle for her.

"Relax, *ma chérie*. The best is yet to come."

She stared into his handsome face, his tension gone and his smile positively lascivious. The impeccable island tycoon garbed in tailored French suits had been replaced by a wild-eyed pirate with seduction oozing from his pores.

Naked and free. And hers.

"Show me," she said.

His smile widened as he let go of the ropes. He dropped, taking her with him, his arms cradling her long before he slammed into the sand.

She straddled him, glorying in the shift of position, of power. The admission was shocking, for she'd never dreamed she'd have sex with a man in the middle of the day on a beach and feel no shame. That she'd revel in being on top.

"The appetizer was wonderful." She dropped a quick kiss on his gorgeous mouth. "What's the entrée?"

"Amour sous le beau ciel."

"I hope that's not fried squid or eyeballs boiled in seaweed."

He threw his head back and laughed, the sound rich and sensual. "Not at all. It means love under the beautiful sky."

"I like that." Especially the love part. For without a doubt, despite everything, she'd fallen hard and fast for André.

She glided her palms up his taut belly, her thumbs tracing the line of black hair that widened over his pectorals. He treated her to much the same torment, sliding his palms up her ribs to cup her breasts.

Their gazes locked, their breaths labored. She stared into eyes that had gone nearly black again. Her fingers danced in an erotic melody over his tanned skin, kneading, marveling at the play of muscle.

She grazed his nipples with her thumbs, dragging a moan from him. Before she could savor her feminine power his hands cupped her breasts, then shifted to tug and roll her nipples between his fingers.

Her mouth opened on a soundless sigh of pleasure, her head tossed back, her world reduced to this moment. This man who knew her body better than she knew it herself.

"About that love under the beautiful sky…" she said, dropping a kiss on his chin, his brow, his nose.

"But of course," he said, between plucking kisses, his voice deep and ragged and oh, so sexy. "Whatever the lady wants."

His heart, she thought. To love and be loved. Now. Forever.

Was that too much to ask? She knew the answer. Knew that it was impossible with him.

His hands shifted to her back, gliding from her behind to her shoulders, kneading the taut muscles in both with such erotic precision she moaned with pleasure and awakened need. Live for the moment, she thought. That was all she could do—all she wanted to do right now.

"I want you," she said, her mouth lowering to his.

She got a fleeting glimpse of longing in his eyes before he jerked his gaze toward the sea. Before she could register that something was wrong, he pushed her down and lunged across her body.

"*Sacre bleu!* Paparazzi."

André yanked a rope on the shelter's post and a bamboo shade unfurled and rolled to the sand. But not before she'd seen the small speedboat bobbing near the shore on a mocha-tinged wash of gold and copper.

Kira flattened on the sand, angry the world had intruded to catch her and André again. How long had they been out there?

André tossed his shirt at her. "Put this on."

She shrugged into it while he stepped into his denim cutoffs. Even with the media drifting dangerously close he left them unbuttoned, seeming content to let them ride low on his lean hips.

He punched numbers into his mobile phone as he hurried her up the slope and into the concealing forest. "Step up the patrol. Paparazzi are offshore at my private beach."

"Don't they ever give up?" she asked, when they'd emerged from the forest and had started toward the house.

"No," he said, giving her a pointed look. "Interesting that they came when we first made love, then again the night you first arrived here, and now."

All times when they'd made love—or nearly. "It's as if they know when we're intimate."

He released a short bark of laughter that sent a chill down her spine. "The same thought crossed my mind, *ma chérie*."

"Do you believe someone is tipping them off?"

"*Oui*—and who among my trusted employees on this small island would betray me?"

She shook her head, having no idea. Then she caught the accusatory glare in his eyes and wanted to retch.

"My God, you can't think that I've alerted the media?"

"Someone has." He opened the door off the back terrace that led directly upstairs and motioned her to precede him.

"It wasn't me," she said, but he merely stared at her.

After the love they'd shared, after isolating her here on Petit St. Marc, he still believed her capable of the impossible. He continued to believe she'd betrayed him, instead of considering that a disgruntled employee had alerted the media.

"If I'd had any means of getting a call out I wouldn't have risked my life rowing to that island today," she said. "I'd have rung my solicitor straightaway and tried to find out who had betrayed *me*."

He shrugged, as if dismissing that possibility. "You could have stowed a cellphone in your luggage."

She jammed her fists at her sides because she truly wanted to cosh him for being so cynical. So arrogantly pig-headed. "I only had one mobile and you took it from me at the Chateau. My God, if you don't believe me, have my room searched."

"It's already been done."

She stepped back, shocked when she shouldn't be surprised. Throughout her days at boarding school everything she'd done, said, or put on paper had been watched. Edouard's orders. Because of his suspicions, shredding paper documents and eliminating electronic ones had become second nature to her— even destroying something as innocuous as jotting down a luncheon date with a friend.

But André's invasion of her privacy had crushed the fragile emotions she held close to her heart. His ordered search of her belongings reminded her that she was a prisoner here. Like her years at boarding school, she was here because of a billionaire's largesse. He didn't trust her or want her.

"You didn't find a mobile phone," she said, the ice of cold reality stabbing her heart when he gave a curt nod. "Have you kept me under surveillance as well?"

His sensuous lips thinned, but his silence was answer enough.

"I'm tired. I need to rest," she said, pushing past him.

Her only thought was fleeing to her room, putting a wall between them when she longed for a continent to divide them. Even then it wouldn't be enough, for André would always be a part of her. Their child would be a constant reminder of what she'd loved. And lost.

She hurried up the stairs. Her feet felt as leaden as her heart, and tears threatened to cloud her vision.

Halfway down the hall her balance deserted her and she stumbled. She pitched forward and threw out her hands to catch herself. Strong arms caught her and swept her off her feet. She gasped, instantly flinging her arms around his neck.

Their eyes clashed. His unreadable. Hers no doubt windows to her soul, her heart.

André broke eye contact first, and the dismissal was another blow in a long line of them.

"Does it bother you to touch someone you distrust so much?" she asked as he carried her to her room, straining away from the welcoming warmth of his chest. The last thing she wanted was his false comfort.

"*Oui.*" He laid her on the bed, then stalked from the room.

Good! She didn't want to be near him. Didn't wish to be subject to his foul mood any longer. But before she could set aside her inner turmoil and will her tense limbs to relax, he returned with a carafe of cold water.

He poured some in a glass and handed it to her. "Drink. I've sent for a doctor."

"That isn't necessary." She took the glass, careful not to touch the fingers that had given her such pleasure an hour before, refusing to look into his eyes and see cold accusation glinting there instead of passion.

"I say it is," he said.

"And, as everyone knows, Monsieur Gauthier's word is law on his island kingdom."

She saluted him with her glass and stared at the wall, her pulse thrumming in time to his harsh indrawn breaths, his shadow looming over her like a dark specter. But she refused to be intimidated—refused to be cowed by him.

"The doctor will be here within the hour," he said.

"Will you stay to oversee his examination?" she asked. "Or watch it through your surveillance cameras?"

"Neither," he said, not denying that monitoring devices were in place, that at some point he had in fact watched her.

Without another word he crossed to the door and shut it with a demoralizing click.

Silence throbbed around her.

Kira closed her eyes, furious. Hurt. Torn by the conflicting emotions clawing for dominance in her heart. She hated him. She loved him.

And loving André Gauthier could destroy her.

After the doctor had visited Kira spent the day in her room, eating and drinking whatever Otillie brought her and attending to a presentation she'd been working on for the Chateau. Though André owned it all now, she needed to see the project through—if only for herself.

She was just putting the finishing touch on it when her door opened. Assuming it was Otillie again, with more food or water, she continued working.

His spicy scent enveloped her a heartbeat before his shadow fell over her. "Is this your renovation plan for the Chateau?"

"Yes. I've been working on it for a month." Likely wasted hours and energy—more dreams crumbling in her grasp.

"I wish to study it."

"You're the boss," she said, trying for a light tone, trying not to feel excited that he was interested in her plans.

If he noticed, he didn't comment as she saved the file to a portable drive and handed it to him. That was when she looked up at him. His powerful aura always took her breath away.

But tonight his dark hair was windblown, and there was a darkly intense gleam in his eyes. He looked as rugged and wild as if he'd just climbed down from the ratlines of a tall ship. And so sexy she trembled with renewed desire.

"You seem pleased with yourself," she said.

"*Oui*. It's begun."

She took a breath, afraid to ask. "What do you mean?"

"Bellamy Enterprises." He tossed the portable drive in the

air and caught it, over and over. "I launched a hostile takeover bid roughly an hour ago."

The breeze drifting through the windows died to a whisper, as if awed by the power he'd wielded. Or perhaps, like her, simply stunned he showed no more excitement over destroying another man's empire. No, not another man—her father.

"You'll control it all, then?" she asked, when she could trust her voice to remain steady. "Blend the two companies into a massive corporation?"

"No. I'll take the dozen or so properties that interest me and sell the rest."

She shook her head, admiring his cunning in the defeat of an adversary. "Peter will have to start all over to acquire half the wealth his father amassed."

"*Oui*. He'll have to earn it."

Which he'd never done. Peter was the heir, whereas she'd had to prove herself to gain her shares in the Chateau.

"Will I have to earn back my position at the Chateau as well?" she asked. "Or have you already dismissed me?"

"I've not replaced you—yet."

She waited for him to go on, to give her an inkling if he would keep her on or let her go, but he simply stared at her, his expression closed. If he shut her out now—

"Does it upset you that I've ruined Peter?" he asked.

"No."

She was certain now that Peter was responsible for selling Edouard's shares in the Chateau, and her own as well. She knew she'd gotten caught in a battle between Peter and André. She knew there was only one way to stop it.

That was the story of her life. In limbo, with neither parent wanting her. She'd lived in the shadow of Edouard Bellamy and his son. She was tired of being a pawn in rich men's games.

That was what she'd been to Edouard. To Peter. And to André, she realized with a sinking heart.

He'd forced her from the Chateau to break Peter, and he'd

crushed her hopes and dreams when he'd seized control of her hotel. Now it was over—or nearly so.

"If you are not grieving for your lover, then why do you look so sad, *ma chérie?*" he asked.

Her lover? If he only knew—

She shook her head, sighed. "Perhaps you are right. I am grieving over the fact that my lover believes I came here to ruin him, that I conspired with his enemy. I'm sad that he believes lies and discounts everything I say."

"The facts are black and white, *ma chérie*. They don't lie."

She'd never win with him. Never. And that realization broke her heart all over again.

"Let me go, André. There's no reason for you to keep me—"

"You are pregnant with my child." He stood over her, as warm and welcoming as a marble statue. "Or is there something you wish to tell me?"

Yes, I am Edouard Bellamy's daughter! The unwanted, unloved, daughter of André's enemy. Get it out in the open. Swiftly. Brutally. Like ripping the bandage off a wound. Then deal with the consequences. And there would be consequences.

If she thought he loved her— If she believed that he could come to love her—

"Answer me, Kira. What are you afraid of?"

She looked up into his mesmerizing eyes and spoke with her heart. "That you'll toss me aside after I've served my purpose to you, when you grow tired of me."

He stared at her a long, charged moment, his body impossibly stiff and unyielding. Then he drew her to him, his head bent so close to hers she saw an inferno of need blazing in his eyes.

"I can't imagine that day ever coming," he said, and captured her mouth with a kiss that seared her to her soul.

She could imagine it coming when she revealed the secret that was festering in her. He'd despise her. She'd be the enemy.

But for the moment she was still his lover. She wanted him

too much to spoil the moment with painful confessions. Just one more night together.

Talk could come later, for it would signal the end she wasn't prepared to make yet. Never mind André had used her—was using her now. She wanted him. She was using him to fill that void.

And, most importantly, she loved him.

It was that simple, and that complex.

She'd pour everything she had into this moment, willing him to believe her, to look into her heart and see the truth. If only she could win his heart, his trust, then maybe the truth wouldn't be so horrible to bear.

And if she was wrong?

She closed her mind to the crippling fear that his hatred would blind him to reason. Blind him to her.

Nothing was stronger than love. She had to believe that.

His long strong fingers entwined with hers as she drew near, the warmth of his touch melting her chilling fears. He brought her hand to his mouth, his eyes ablaze with passion. The kiss he pressed into her palm fired her with heat and she trembled with guilt and anticipation.

He escorted her into his room and peeled off his shorts. Her body quivered at the sight of him, warmed her skin and her heart, for he was beautifully sculpted, his tanned skin stretched smooth over chiseled muscles gleaming like bronze.

"You are magnificent," she said.

"I am just a man." He took her clothes from her, then dropped kisses on the flesh he'd exposed. "But you are a goddess of pleasure and beauty."

His compliment needled her conscience, for she was a goddess who'd kept something vital from him.

He trailed kisses up her arms, his breath hot against her skin, his body burning her where it touched. Hot, cold. Fiery passion, cold reality.

She opened her mouth, guilt spoiling her pleasure. Her confession was poised on her tongue. But his mouth fused to hers, his kisses an addiction she could never get enough of.

"Only in your arms," she said. But how long could this passion last?

A lifetime wouldn't be long enough, she admitted, as his hands played a lusty symphony on her breasts while his teeth nipped at her collarbone, her neck. She clung to his broad shoulders and let her head fall back, surrendering to him.

He made a rough sound in his throat and tugged her into his *en suite* bathroom. And he proceeded to teach her a whole new appreciation for high-dollar French water jets.

In the small hours of the morning André sprawled in bed with Kira snuggled to his side. He should have fallen asleep shortly after she had, but slumber had eluded him.

Their lovemaking had been intense, passionate, deeper than he'd ever experienced in his life. He'd deliberately avoided talk, for he planned to spend the night making love with lazy abandon—a rich dessert to savor in nibbles and bites after a sumptuous meal. To celebrate. To seduce. To delight in each touch, each kiss, each joining.

But he'd sensed a desperation in Kira that had left him on edge. As if she feared this would be the last time they'd make love. A time or two he'd glimpsed guilt in her eyes.

Oui, she was keeping some secret, one that was causing her anguish. The likely scenario ate at him like acid.

The baby was Bellamy's—not his. Despite the passion they found in each other's arms she would chose Bellamy over him. She'd betray his trust and make a fool out of him again.

André set his jaw, anger tensing muscle and tendon, eroding the exquisite pleasure he'd found in her arms. Pleasure he'd never experienced to this extent with another woman!

Even knowing she'd been Peter's mistress, he wanted her for himself. The admission came hard. He hated to be so captivated by a woman that he'd debate even for a second considering having something more than an affair with her.

But the brutal fact remained that he wanted Kira as his lover, his wife. As the mother of *his* children. He would give her anything she whimpered for to please her. He wanted her child to be his.

But if it wasn't?

The guilt he'd sensed in her burned like acid in him, for it could only mean one thing. She'd already been carrying Bellamy's child when she'd first come here to deceive him. His enemy was the father of her baby.

Mon Dieu, she was the fire that coursed through his blood. The siren who invaded his thoughts. She'd made a soft home in his hardened heart.

He wanted her. Now and forever.

But he couldn't—*wouldn't!*—claim Bellamy's child. Admitting that pained him as nothing else had, and if that was her secret he'd lose Kira forever.

He should be relieved. When he was free of her he'd regain control of his life, his emotions.

He would escape the silken trap that had destroyed his father. He wouldn't become intoxicated by a conniving woman, rendered drunk by her essence.

He would escape this affair with his pride and honor, leaving with only a few scars to his heart. They'd heal. He'd forget her. He would.

Then he'd be rid of this driving need to cover her luscious body with kisses, to sink into her welcoming heat and forget the world. Like he ached to do now.

He lurched from the bed and crossed to the window, refusing to heed her siren's call, offering him the sweetest nectar of the gods. It was a trap, for her kind lured men to their ruin.

André heard the slither of silken sheets on the bed and tensed, willed her to stay there even though his body begged her to come to him. He'd be strong. Unyielding. Resistant to her charms.

"Is something wrong?" she asked, her voice soft and sexy.

"No." He flattened a palm on the windowsill, staring out into the night when every cell in his body ached to return to the bed. To her.

"I don't believe you."

His mouth pulled in a mocking smile, and he applauded her for her insight. "Go back to sleep."

"I'd rather talk."

Talk was the last thing he wanted to do. He didn't wish to hear her confession. Didn't wish to end this idyll.

A sudden gust of wind sent the filmy curtains fluttering over his heated skin like feathers, filling the room with whispers of the dark desires he'd run from all his life.

He was lost and he knew it, because he still wanted her. Standing here wouldn't change that. Perhaps she was right. Perhaps it was time they talked. Then she'd know what he was willing to give her, and what he'd never be able to relinquish.

"Very well. What is it you wish to say?"

He heard her shaky indrawn breath, and took satisfaction at knowing she was as off balance as he felt.

"What did Edouard do to merit your vengeance?" she asked.

Mon Dieu, she dared to bring Bellamy into their bed?

André whirled to face her, his body taut with anger. "I told you—he destroyed my family."

"How?"

"C'est sans importance!"

"Speak English!"

He made a slashing movement with his hand and stalked across the room. "It's not important. Nothing can change the past."

Because if it had been possible he would have done so. He wouldn't have told his father what his headstrong sister had done. He held himself to blame for setting in motion the events that had led to his parents' deaths and his own abandonment.

"Please. I want to know," she said. "I must know."

He looked at her then, and a good deal of his rage cooled. She was huddled against the headboard, the sheet pulled tight around her. Even in the wan moonlight her face looked unnaturally pale.

Looking at her, he had trouble believing this woman with scruples had conspired with Peter to gain control of Edouard's empire—that, like his sister, she'd done whatever a Bellamy wanted on the promise of inheriting the Chateau. Kira had come here to seduce him when his defenses had been at their lowest. Like his sister, she'd chosen a Bellamy over him.

How could he ever forgive her for that? He didn't know if he could, and that realization had him tied in hard knots.

"André?" she asked. "Please?"

"My sister was Edouard's mistress," he began. "Seduced by him when she was fifteen."

She jerked her gaze from his, staring at the wall as if enthralled by watching a drama play out. When she spoke, her voice was a pained hush that vibrated along his raw nerves. "You hate him for stealing her innocence, then?"

"*Oui*, it started then," he said, and then wondered if anyone had given a damn when Bellamy had taken Kira from the schoolroom and become her benefactor.

He had proof of it even if she denied it. Even though she had ended up becoming Peter's mistress.

"What's the rest?"

He shook his head, bitten with guilt that his concern now rested with Kira instead of his family. Even admitting it didn't change anything, for he suspected she'd been an easy target.

She should be the last person he'd wish to share his deepest grief and guilt with. Not the one woman he wanted to talk to about his tragic past.

"It's complicated," he said.

"Most intrigues are. Please go on."

"My parents were outraged and forbade Suzette to see

Edouard," he said, frowning as memories of his parents' heated arguments filtered back to him. "But my sister was charmed by Edouard's wealth, by his promises of showering her with riches."

"And Edouard was relentless in his pursuit of her?" she said, accurately guessing that much.

"*Oui*. One night she ran away." He shook his head, having relived that event a thousand times in his nightmares. "I was twelve, and I took great pleasure rushing to let my father know."

She swallowed, the sound loud in the tense stillness. "Did he go after her?"

He stiffened, his hands fisting. "No, my mother did. My father jumped in the car to stop her, for her driving was atrocious. They never made it down the mountain."

She winced, pinching her eyes shut. "And your sister?"

"I learned later that Edouard was waiting to whisk Suzette away to America." To the Chateau Mystique. He stared at her, letting her see the anguish and torment he'd lived with for years.

"What happened to you after your parents died?"

"I was shipped off to a distant relative."

"Then you were raised by family?"

André laughed—the sound as cold and calculating as his mother's conniving cousin. Only by the grace of God and his own determination had he survived.

"They didn't want me, *ma chérie*, but they gladly accepted the monthly allowance they were given to keep me."

"I know how difficult that kind of life is."

"You can't begin to guess. While you were taking your lessons at an elite boarding school, I was working when the local school wasn't in session."

He glanced out the window at the bloated moon, the pain of being shuffled off to strangers still festering under the service. He'd had a roof over his head, a small closet-like room with a cot to call his own, and food that had been better fitted for the swine raised on the farm.

"Who provided your allowance?" she asked, her voice small.

"Edouard Bellamy. He paid them to keep me out of his and Suzette's way."

André had counted the days until he could escape that hell. Marked time toward the day he would ruin Edouard Bellamy.

"I'm so sorry," she said.

"Don't be." He didn't want her pity. Nor would he admit how deep those scars cut—how much he blamed himself for telling his father what his sister had done. "Suzette made her choice. I made mine."

How ironic that Edouard and Suzette had died after a horrible car wreck. Poetic justice? Perhaps.

"Why can't you give up your vengeance?" Kira asked.

"Pride. *Le code d'honneur*," he said, and when she slid him a questioning look added, "My honor demands I avenge those who have wronged my family."

She shook her head, looking rather appalled. "That's it? You vowed to ruin Edouard because your sister willingly became his mistress?"

Mon Dieu, she made it sound trivial. "There is more to it than that."

He drove his fingers through his hair, loath to talk about his parents. They'd been spoiled and rich, living for the moment in whatever spotlight shone on them. They had been ill suited to raise a family or manage their wealth.

André reasoned it had been only a matter of time before his parents made a powerful enemy. Not surprisingly, it had been his mother who'd played a dangerous game with Edouard Bellamy—all to make her husband jealous enough to cease his wanderings.

He doubted either parent had realized Edouard Bellamy was vindictive to a fault. That when Bellamy realized he'd been played for a fool he'd ruthlessly lured André's father into bankruptcy and André's sister into his bed.

"André?" she asked. "What happened? Tell me."

"My father built the Chateau Mystique for my mother," he

said. "His gift to her. Before it was completed Bellamy set out
to acquire it by dubious means. I am merely reclaiming what
belonged to my family and restoring our honor."

She stared at him for the longest time, then lifted her hands
and clapped, the sound obscene in the tense stillness. "Bravo,
André. You have accomplished what you set out to do in the name
of honor by employing dubious means—just like Edouard."

He bristled, hating the comparison. Hating that she was
right. But at least he wasn't alone.

"Look in the mirror, *ma chérie*. You came here to do Peter
Bellamy's bidding. You are the one *enceinte*. Or have you so
quickly forgotten the role you played for him three months ago?"

She scooted from the bed, her face ashen. "I'm going to my
room to sleep. The ghosts in here make it too crowded."

André took a step forward to stop her, then stilled the urge.
The timing was bad. He'd only dig a bigger hole for himself if
he pulled her back to him as he longed to do. If he kissed her.
Loved her. Sought comfort in her arms.

His emotions were too raw. Tomorrow, he thought, as she
left the bedroom without looking back.

Tomorrow he'd have total control of Bellamy Enterprises—
and of Kira Montgomery.

CHAPTER EIGHT

KIRA curled in a ball on her bed, too heartbroken to cry. What good would tears do now?

Her father hadn't just crushed André's family. Edouard had ripped André away from everything he'd known. Everyone he'd loved. He'd somehow acquired the Chateau—the hotel André's father had built for his mother—and he'd ensconced André's sister there as his mistress.

She understood André's agony, his rage, for she'd lived with something similar herself. Only it had been her own mother who'd abandoned her to Edouard's care, and his brand of accepting responsibility had been to ship her off to boarding school in England.

From the day she'd first met Edouard he'd referred to her as his "shameful obligation." She'd believed herself inferior to his legitimate family. Insignificant. And always unwanted.

To think she'd tried so hard to win Edouard's favor, his attention, as a child hungry for affection. To think she'd been so desperate for love that she'd agreed to keep her paternity a secret all her life. That she'd never gone against Edouard's wishes and contacted his "real" family.

Yes, she and André had both suffered at Edouard Bellamy's hands, though she feared André would not view her experience the same way. Because she was a Bellamy, and there was nothing she could do about that.

A man like André did not forgive deceit. And she'd deceived him. Was still deceiving him.

Her hands glided over her belly, cradling the life that grew there. She should've told him the truth from the start. Gotten it out in the open before she lost her heart to him. Let her ghosts dance and rattle their chains along with his.

But she hadn't, because postponing the inevitable was easier than facing the truth. Because she was afraid to trust that he'd do the right thing. Because she didn't want anything to throw a pall over their passionate tryst on this island. She wanted to prolong the inevitable.

Now she was too tired to think straight—too exhausted from spent passion and from the tangled dreams she'd spun of her and André and their child. She was simply too heavy of heart to risk seeing the thin thread binding them snap in two.

She'd seek him out in the morning and tell him everything, for the guilt of lying to him was tearing her apart. She had to believe that love was stronger than hate.

André had been hunched over his desk since dawn, gaze fixed on the computer screen. The work he'd hoped to immerse himself in this morning stared back at him. The latest financial report was a jumble of words, none making sense. The spread-sheet might as well be random figures.

All he could think about was Kira and the stricken look on her face when she'd left his bedroom. He'd shocked her by admitting he was Suzette's brother, and shocked himself by revealing so much about his family's connection to Edouard Bellamy. None of his contemporaries knew. Not one. So why had he trusted Kira with the truth?

He caught a subtle whiff of her perfume a heartbeat before his door opened a crack. His gaze flicked from the wealth of auburn hair to her eyes that gleamed with moisture.

"Are you too busy to talk?" she asked.

He was, and talk was the last thing he wanted to do with

her—especially if she was emotional. But he didn't wish to turn her away either.

"Come in," he said, rising and hoping she wouldn't hear his heart slamming against his ribs. "What's on your mind?"

She slipped inside like a shadow and closed the door, her eyes seeming too large for her face. She swallowed, looked away, then met his gaze again.

"Something you said last night…" She waved a hand in a classic gesture of nervousness and eased onto the chair, but sat on its edge as if ready to bolt. "I've never told anyone before."

"A confession, then?"

"A secret, actually."

His gut clenched, but he erased all emotion from his face. This was it. The declaration of guilt he'd dreaded to hear. Their affair would end swiftly and unpleasantly.

She took a deep breath. Expelled it slowly. His gut clenched again. He was dreading what truth would spill from her lush lips.

"My mother was a Las Vegas showgirl and my father—" She frowned. Swallowed. Paled. "My father—"

He took pity on her struggle for a way to tell him. "I've seen your birth certificate and I know you are illegitimate."

A flush kissed her cheeks, but he couldn't tell if it was from embarrassment or anger. "Yes, my mother obviously wasn't sure which was one of her lovers was my father when she gave birth to me."

He stared at her, stunned for a heartbeat. In his mind he'd pictured her mother as a quiet Englishwoman, reserved and withdrawn. He'd imagined Kira had run away from the staid life she'd been born into to the glamour Bellamy promised.

"Your mother sent you to England to be schooled, then?" Away from the lurid nightlife and her liaisons?

A deeper red tinted her delicate cheekbones, and he knew at that moment that no matter what she told him she'd seen more than a young girl should. "She gave me up when I was quite young. Actually, I barely remember her."

"Is she still alive?"

"I wouldn't know."

"You've never tried to find her?"

"No, and I never will."

André wasn't sure what to make of that admission. Kira was compassionate to a fault. She wouldn't cut her mother from her life without just cause—that cause being that the woman had obviously placed her lovers before her child. Yet Kira had followed in the woman's footsteps—unmarried and pregnant.

But where her mother had obviously been derelict in her duty, André believed Kira would make a fine parent. He trusted she'd cherish her child. His soul knew she'd put her child first, even above him. He trusted her with the care of their baby.

He shook his head, keeping the last observation to himself. "I take it you were adopted?"

"No, I was simply a ward." She looked at him then, the lonely ache of her childhood plain to see, touching his heart as nothing else ever had. "As I said before, I know how you felt, being foisted off on people who cared nothing for you."

For a moment he thought she'd expand on her upbringing, but she stopped talking and frowned.

"Then you understand why I must bring down everything Bellamy built," he said.

"No, I don't understand that at all," she said.

She couldn't mean that. "I don't believe you haven't thought of ways to make your mother pay for abandoning you. Or wanted to lash out at the guardian who closeted you away instead of welcoming you into a family."

Kira looked away, but not before he caught a flicker of anger in her expressive eyes. "I locked my ghosts away long ago. I knew to dwell on what I couldn't change would turn me bitter and ultimately destroy me."

He sensed there was more, that she was holding something back, something that she was hesitant to divulge. He understood her reluctance, for he suspected she had never allowed herself to be angry at the cloistered life meted out to her. She'd been conditioned to accept her fate.

"Will it help if you tell me about your ghosts?" he asked. "I assure you I'm not one to fear them."

"André," she said, her face too pale and too drawn.

André waited for her to go on, but she fell silent.

Mon Dieu! He longed to rip open the shroud on her past, to make whoever had hurt her pay for their callous disregard. He wanted to hold her and love her and promise her all would be well—that he'd slay her dragons too.

But he couldn't bring himself to step over that last fence. For, like her, he wasn't accustomed to divulging any of his secrets—especially personal ones.

They had the power to cause heartache. To draw blood.

Oui, he couldn't totally trust her. But he could offer an olive branch.

"I read over your plans for the Chateau and I applaud your foresight," he said.

Her expressive eyes went wide, and her smile brightened the room and his heart. "You did?"

"But of course that's not what I wish to discuss now. I'd like your opinion concerning a resort I plan to redesign in Cap d'Antibes," he said, turning his attention to the spreadsheet on the computer. Her radiant expression had burst inside him like the sun cresting the horizon, flooding him with new hopes, new dreams. It made him forget his quest for vengeance.

"Are you familiar with the area?" he asked, his voice sharper than intended.

"Only what I've read about the French Riviera," she said.

He'd take her there. Give her a tour of the old city from a native's viewpoint. Show her the castle steeped in history and the villas where movie stars and royalty spent their holidays.

He'd escort her to the casinos that never slept. Then do something he'd never done before—take a lover to the old villa where he'd been born.

"Please—tell me more." She shifted in her seat, her eyes still wide with excitement.

Mon Dieu, to think his business enthused her so! To think her excitement was rubbing off on him—in more ways than one.

"I recently bought the hotel. It's a fine property, but the last modernization stripped it of its charm." He leaned forward, captivated by her interest. "I would like to reinstall its original nineteen-forties style."

She sat back, her expression thoughtful. "You want to recapture its heyday?"

"Oui." André rocked back in his chair, then tossed his pen on the desk, as if it didn't matter whether she liked his idea or not. It did matter. He'd seen her credentials and knew she had a head for business.

"It's daring. Unique." She smiled, and his heart nearly stopped beating. "And a cutting-edge business strategy."

"I'll show you the plans—" His mobile phone chirped and he answered it.

"Bonjour," said the manager of La Cachette, his high-class resort on St. Barthélemy. *"Comment allez-vous?"*

"I am well. To what do I owe the pleasure?"

"A small matter, really." The manager explained that there was a continuing problem with an employee—André's distant cousin.

"Philippe is not doing his job?" André asked.

"No, his work is excellent." There was a long, tense pause. "It is the ladies. He romances them, and there are complaints."

André smiled at the mental image that conjured. "So Philippe is working his way through the female employees, *non*?"

"Employees, guests—it makes no difference to him. Complaints have been lodged." His manager's sigh crackled over the line. "Perhaps if you spoke with him?"

"Oui. I will arrive this afternoon. Prepare my suite."

André ended the connection, then rocked back in his chair and pinched the bridge of his nose, annoyed he had to speak with Philippe again about his discretion and maintaining high business standards. Irked he had to leave Kira here. Though a night away from her might be just the thing to put his emotions back in perspective.

"Problems?" Kira's voice reached across the desk to stroke over him in a silken caress.

"*Oui*. An ongoing one." But no more. His cousin had been warned what would happen if he continued to play around.

He met her gaze, annoyed her excitement had vanished. Was she sorry to see him go, or was it a ruse?

No, she wasn't deceiving him this time. He'd set out to bind her to him and he'd succeeded. But he'd not anticipated his plan would ensnare him as well.

He should leave her here and attend to business. But he self-ishly wanted her to join him.

"We leave for St. Barth within the hour," he said, clearly surprising her again.

Again her smile dazzled him, warming something that had been far too cold in him. "You're taking me?"

"But of course."

Her smile rivaled the sun.

Oui, she was excited to go away with him for the day. He hoped she wanted to see the island and La Cachette—to be alone with him in the romantic city. But she might be seeing this as her chance to contact Peter, perhaps even run away.

His jaw firmed, his heart chilling at those possibilities. He'd provide her with the means to deceive him. He'd charge his investigator to do a deeper investigation of her, turning over every rock in England if need be.

Then he'd have an answer. Then he'd know what the hell to do.

Kira wasn't a neophyte when it came to five-star hotels, but the moment André escorted her into his hotel on St. Barth, there was something about La Cachette that set it apart from anything she'd seen before. Something besides the old-world beauty of the salmon-stucco structure trimmed in pristine white. Something other than what she'd read about the high-end suites that ran into many thousands of dollars a night.

The elegant hotel overlooking the expanse of turquoise sea made Chateau Mystique pale in comparison. It reduced the Chateau to what it really was—a glitzy hotel on the Las Vegas strip, an edifice of glass and steel and opulence meant to dazzle guests, like countless other ones in the neon town that played all night long.

Her nerves zinged and her senses absorbed the grandeur of it all as André tapped in a code to access a private lift. But once she and André stepped inside it, a far different excitement took root in her.

She'd been intimate with him in every way possible, yet she felt like an exposed novice trembling at his side. A good part of it was because of desire, for she wanted him with a hunger that shocked her.

But she was still shaken over taking the coward's way out and holding her secret to her heart even after he'd asked for her opinion regarding his property on the French Riviera. At that moment she'd felt their relationship shift, and she hadn't wanted to ruin it. And it had happened again when he'd offered that bit of praise for her ideas for the Chateau.

Her heart had melted.

After three months they'd gone from captive and captor, to sizzling lovers. Could they find even ground in a partnership in business? As parents?

Could they have even more?

She wanted to believe it was possible—that he'd not hold her paternity against her or their child. That he'd brought her to St. Barth not just because she was his willing mistress now.

She had to trust her heart that love would find a way.

That was so easy to do now, as his dark eyes glittered with blatant desire, caressing her in tantalizing increments. Her lips tingled, aching for his kiss. Her breasts felt heavy, tight, and her blood hummed with a strong sensual pulse.

His powerful presence filled the lift, filled her heart. She'd never met a man who captivated her so, who made her ache for such wicked pleasure in his arms.

Though the lift had whisked them to the penthouse, she was gasping for breath, her hand gripping the cool handrail as his gaze fixed on the juncture of her thighs. A deep throb of want vibrated low in her belly, her muscles contracting in erotic rhythm.

The apex of her thighs was growing hot, the scent of her sex making her cheeks warm more from arousal than embarrassment. She squirmed, as restless as if he'd touched her intimately.

The flames in his gaze blazed hotter. His wickedly sensual lips curved in a knowing smile—a triumphant smile, for he surely knew the power he had over her.

As if to prove it he licked his lips and moaned his pleasure. A tremor rocked through her and she pressed her thighs tight together, nearly coming in the lift, aroused simply by his gaze, by the carnal promise in his dark eyes.

With just one look she was lost. She was his.

He knew it, and so did she.

The lift door whispered open. André wrapped an arm around her shoulders and escorted her into the tower apartment, no doubt aware her legs trembled so badly she feared she'd collapse.

She'd expected him to whisk her to the bedroom, but he seemed in no particular hurry. If only *she* could be that relaxed.

Kira focused on the suite to calm her emotions. She'd not expected the apartment's style to be so starkly elegant.

Open, yet intimate. The ultimate playpen for decadence.

Large windows on three sides welcomed sunlight to flood the open salon, which was sumptuously dressed in translucent swaths of lush green that mirrored the colors of the rainforest.

The curved sectional sofa in a warm butterscotch dominated the salon, affording an optimum view of the ocean and the vista stretching to the horizon. Her mind teased her with images of her and André frolicking on that sofa, having eyes only for each other.

An intimate glass-topped table for two sat by French doors that opened onto a white-railed Juliet balcony. A crystal vase overflowed with white lilies, cream isianthus and eucalyptus foliage to perfume the suite.

Her gaze climbed the curved staircase to the loft above. With André so close, and knowing what was to come, this was almost too much for her senses.

"The bedroom," he said.

"Of course." She studied the open plan again, noting one closed door on this level. "Are there others?"

"No."

Her face flushed. She should be offended he'd brought her here. But all she could think of was making love with him on the plush sofa, and later in the tower bedroom.

"Do you want anything?" he asked.

She wanted him to take her now, to pleasure her—love her. "You," she said simply.

An amorous glint lit his eyes. "Ah, *ma chérie*, you do speak my language. Unfortunately I have pressing business to attend to now."

She crossed to him and laid a hand on his heart, emboldened by the strong rapid beat, unwilling to conform to the mistress's role of waiting patiently for her lover. "When will you return?"

"An hour. Two at the most."

A short time for him, but a boring afternoon for her. "Perhaps I'll take advantage of the solitude and do a bit of shopping."

"No—not with the paparazzi lingering."

Her first impulse was to react with anger, but she didn't want to confront the media. "Very well, I'll stay here."

"I'll make your wait worth it." His mouth closed over hers, hot, hungry, possessive.

She kissed him in kind, willing him to remember the promise awaiting him here. Willing him to hurry back to her.

He pulled back too soon, his eyes black with passion, his face taut. "Make yourself at home." Then he was gone, disappearing into the lift and leaving her alone.

Kira stared at the green light on the lift's keypad. He'd not locked it. Had he forgotten?

No, he wasn't one to make that type of error. He'd left it unlocked for a reason. But what was it?

Kira fetched a bottle of sparkling water from the small refrigerator in the kitchen and paced the lavish salon, wondering if this was a test of her loyalty to him.

Could it be as simple as him knowing she wouldn't go shopping and draw the media's attention? Could he know she wouldn't run away from him? Know that when he returned this evening she'd be here waiting for him?

Either way he trusted her—or at least had begun to.

She set the water aside and wrapped her arms around her middle, sick at heart that her secret would destroy that newfound trust. But even if she could prove she hadn't conspired with Peter to ruin André, there was still the fact she was Edouard Bellamy's daughter.

There was nothing she could do to forestall the inevitable. How much better it would've been to have lost him then rather than now. How much more heartache could she bear?

His avowal as they waited out the storm in the cave on Noir Creux came back to her. *It's too late. I paid your price.*

But he didn't know she'd been deceived, and she had nothing but her word to change his mind.

Kira crossed to the phone and quickly dialed the number of her solicitor. Her frustration hitched up another notch when the hotel operator answered.

"Pardon? I don't understand," Kira said.

The woman replied in French—then hung up on her! So much for placing a call.

She reclaimed her water and climbed the steps to the tower bedroom, her weariness eased marginally by the breathtaking view afforded by the bank of windows. No matter where she looked, her gaze fell on the sea.

A massive bed dressed simply and elegantly in jade and black dominated the space. She gripped her bottled water tighter, her body quivering with need. This was insane.

Her world was on the verge of collapsing and she was fantasizing about making love with him. Was she following in her mother's footsteps?

No! She'd put her child first, even above her own needs.

She'd turned to descend to the main salon when she noticed a small desk set in an alcove near the far side of the room. It held a laptop computer and nothing else. *Make yourself at home.*

Doing just that, she sent a quick missive to her solicitor, demanding to know who'd forged her signature for the sale of her stock.

Time inched by as she waited on pins and needles for his reply. Alert, wary, and plagued with new guilt.

Her hands fisted. My God, how deeply André had woven her into his web if she felt guilty for contacting her solicitor about the takeover of the Chateau.

A soft tone issued from the computer as the "new mail" icon flashed on, seeming unnaturally loud in the stillness. She frowned as she read the reply from her solicitor.

He'd been forthright with her from the beginning, a loyal employee of Edouard's. She'd trusted him without question.

But his cryptic reply worried her. Instead of answering her questions, he asked what game she was playing now?

She'd never played any game—that had been her father's forte. Not hers. She'd been taken to Petit St. Marc against her will. She'd been robbed of her shares!

A ding below stairs alerted her that the lift had come up. She typed a quick response to her solicitor, telling him to explain in detail what he meant. She reiterated again that *she* was the injured party here. She'd never authorized the sale of her stock. Never. She wanted answers, and she wanted them now.

She'd find a way to read his reply later. And if she couldn't…?

Kira logged off just as the tap of shoes on tile echoed up from below. André had returned sooner than she'd expected.

She ran into the bedroom, then hesitated, knowing if she rushed down the steps that she'd either look guilty or eager to see him. She latched on to the latter, but when she got to the top of the stairs she froze.

It wasn't André at all, but a woman. Her uniform was clearly that of a domestic. She set a box held tight with a crimson bow on the table and turned to leave, then stopped and looked up at Kira, as if sensing her there watching.

"Bonjour, mademoiselle," the woman said, and smiled. "A gift for you. *Monsieur* apologizes for being detained."

"André sent me a gift?"

"Oui." The maid walked back toward the lift.

Curiosity carried Kira down the stairs. The maid was gone before she reached the salon. She read the note attached to the box.

Instead of returning to Petit St. Marc this evening they would enjoy a dinner at the celebrated La del'Impératrice Chambre.

The fact her casual clothes were unsuitable for the elite restaurant barely registered. All she could think of was spending the night in that massive bed with André, loving him.

Heat spread across her middle, fanning out in delicious shivers. They'd enjoy dinner out, like a real date, then spend the night here.

Kira's hands shook as she tore open the box and swept ivory tissue aside. Her gaze lit on a silky blue fabric that caught the light and shimmered like sunrays skipping over the Caribbean waters.

She held it up, as excited as a child at Christmas. It was indecent. Seductive. Daring. She'd never worn anything like this—had never even tried on risqué clothes.

But André had chosen this for her. The reason was clear.

She was his mistress. He wanted to show her off—boast to other men that she was his possession, his kept woman. She was his conquest over Peter Bellamy.

Her excitement dimmed as that fact stole away the glow she'd been basking in. It would end soon, for she couldn't go on avoiding the inevitable much longer.

Kira dropped her gaze to the designer gown clutched in her hands. She couldn't wear it and keep her self-respect. But she couldn't resist trying it on either. Just once.

She was about to retreat upstairs when a scrap of color in the box caught her eye. No, he hadn't—

But he had.

She picked up the flesh-hued scrap of silk that was panties. They felt like heaven in her hand but were surely devilish in design, for the cloth was transparent.

She might as well be wearing none at all! No doubt André had thought the same when he'd bought them.

The square box that accompanied the larger one had to be shoes. Curious to see what he'd chosen, she slipped the ribbon free and flung off the lid.

Her hand trembled as she lifted one beautiful mermaid sandal from the box. Shoes were her passion. Her weakness. And these sexy stilettoes called to her.

What would it hurt to try the entire outfit on, as he'd intended her to do? Nothing. André wouldn't return for hours. Nobody would know. Nobody but her.

Flushed and excited at the prospect of being that audacious—even in private!—she rushed upstairs to don the daring dress. The second it slid over her body she felt wicked and sensual. And horribly self-conscious.

The design was pure seduction. Thin strips of fabric covered her breasts and tied behind the neck, leaving her back bare nearly to the swell of her buttocks.

The silk caressed her with each step, each breath, the glide over her nipples teasing them erect, the whisper of cloth over her hips and thighs keeping her senses tuned to a high pitch.

Just like André's hands and mouth would do.

She swallowed hard, near panting with desire. She'd never felt this sexually attractive in her life. Never been so aware of herself as a woman.

Kira allowed herself one last look in the mirror, scarce believing that temptress was her. But her bare feet ruined the effect. Damn, she'd left the sandals downstairs.

She glanced at the clock, sure she had time to try on the shoes. She hurried down the stairs and did just that. The fit was perfect, like a fairy tale.

Another ding rang through the apartment. She froze, her gaze locked on the lift door. Her stomach quivered; her pulse hammered. She knew André had arrived even before the door whispered open and he stepped from the lift.

She had no idea where he'd acquired the elegantly cut black tuxedo, or where he'd shaved, but he looked like a page torn from a designer magazine. He looked like the fantasy in every erotic dream she'd ever had. The essence of *savoir-faire*.

It was one of the few French phrases that had stuck with her. Oddly appropriate as André possessed social grace and aplomb. And a sensuality that seduced her across the room, robbing her of all thoughts save one—making love with him.

He strode into the salon and stopped, freezing in place like a mannequin, with a hand poised to smooth back his dark hair. His gaze locked on hers, hot and hungry.

Her stomach flip-flopped, tightening. Her thighs clenched. Her breasts felt full, the sensation of her nipples peaking against the silk almost too much to bear.

Her heart quivered, overflowing with love. Love?

Yes, I love him.

Forever. Fatalistically.

She smiled with all her heart and strode toward him, hating that she was continuing her deception. But she didn't want to ruin this night either.

Tonight she'd be his willing lover. She'd love him as if there was no tomorrow. Because when the truth came out she feared there would be no future for them. She knew putting off telling the truth didn't change it.

But when she did this affair would be over. Her life, her hopes, her dreams with André would end.

And when they did a part of her would die.

André's chest was so tight he could barely draw air into his lungs. When he did manage it, he drew in the floral scent she wore as well as her womanly essence.

He'd known when he bought the gown that the sapphire silk would complement Kira's wealth of auburn hair, known that the fabric would caress her full breasts, hug her lush hips, and glide down the expanse of strong shapely legs like his hands and mouth longed to do.

She was a vixen. The colors of the sea and the sand and temptation. A lover molded just for him.

And for Bellamy?

His hands fisted, his gut twisting, for he didn't want his enemy to shadow him tonight. Not now, when this strange warmth was spreading over his chest, filling him with a sense of rightness.

For the first time in his life he had found a woman he wanted in all ways—as his lover, the mother of his children. As his wife?

Mon Dieu, he couldn't marry Peter's mistress. But the idea of another man touching Kira enraged him. His hungry gaze swept over her, stripping off the dress that set his blood on fire. His fingers tingled to put action to the thought.

Every man who saw her would feel the same. His gut clenched at the certainty. He'd be damned if he'd share her.

No one would see her luscious curves in that dress but him! Nobody but him would touch her, kiss her, desire her.

He would be the last lover she'd ever take, because it must be so.

It *was* so! He knew that now. Mother and child were his. *His!*

André strode toward her, his hunger for food gone, replaced by a carnal appetite that was stronger. He'd have her now. Hear his name on her lips as she climaxed. See her smile rest on his face before sleep claimed her.

Now and always.

He pulled her to him, his finesse shattering like fine crystal, his patience vanishing like smoke. "Our plans have changed. We will stay here."

"Good," she said, lifting her face to his. "I would just as soon order room service."

"*Oui*, a late dinner," he said, gliding his hands down her bare back, watching her beautiful eyes gleam with the same powerful desire that raged through him. "Much later."

She was a worthy partner for him, capable of bringing him low with one innocent look, causing his blood to race out of control with that bed-me gleam in her eyes. Like they had now, her head bent just so, her tongue caressing her lips and making him crazy with want.

She was his to have. Without doubt. Without reservation.

André claimed her mouth, vowing he'd soon hold her heart and soul in his hands as well. She melded against him, capitulating to his sensual siege, her mouth surrendering.

Each stroke of her tongue fanned the flames of his passion, until he feared he'd spend himself here in the salon. He who always maintained control felt it crack as her greedy hands explored his torso and caressed his hips, her thumbs tracing over the ridge at his flanks, feeling like fire and ice and sweet, sweet heaven.

He swept his palms over her rounded hips, certain the finest satins and silks could not compare to the exquisite smoothness of her skin. The deep valley of her spine invited him to follow it in minute measures down to the soft swell of her bottom.

The gown was no barrier as he dipped his hands beneath the indecently low back and splayed his fingers over her satiny flesh, barely covered with the minuscule triangle of silk.

He smiled, pleased she'd worn his gift. For him. Only him.

She arched against him, her fingers wadding his shirt, the scrape of her nails sending fire licking through him.

He heard the rending of fabric, then sucked in great gulps of air as her palms swept over his bare chest, her thumbs brushing his nipples. "Aggression becomes you, *ma chérie*."

"I want you naked, André. I want to feel you moving on me. In me."

The growl that escaped him was foreign, feral. He swept her into his arms and mounted the stairs, their mouths straining at the other, their lips dueling with fierce intent.

They fell onto the bed, tearing at their clothes, thousands of dollars' worth of silk rendered to rags. He moved over her, his sex tight and hard, poised at her moist cay.

"Yes," she said, grabbing his sides. "Now."

"Not yet."

He palmed her breasts as his mouth moved down her body, tasting, teasing. She cried out his name, arching her back as if desperate to impale herself on him.

But that pleasure would come too soon. Too rushed to be appreciated at this moment in time.

He hooked his thumbs under the lace banding her panties and pulled them off by inches, his heart slamming hard as her scent filled his nostrils, driving him wild.

"André!" The reedy sound of his name on her lips roared through him like flame. "Please."

He would. By God, he would please her. In her pleasure he'd find his own reward.

His breath rasped hard as he tossed aside her panties, his patience with obstacles and leisurely sex gone. She was gasping for air as well, her beautiful body bared to his hungry eyes, her lush breasts thrust forward, the nipples peaked, her sleek legs parted in wanton invitation.

"You are exquisite," he said, his palms sliding up her legs to the dark curls at the apex of her thighs.

She grabbed for him, her fingers gliding off his slick chest, her eyes dark with passion. "Kiss me."

And he did, bending his head to the heat of her, his fingers spreading her as his tongue flicked over her damp swollen flesh, certain nothing on earth was as delicious as she.

Mewling sounds came from her as her fingers twined in his hair and pulled, but he blocked out the slight pain and continued his ruthless oral seduction of her.

He laved her once, twice, his own need close to the edge, his fingers slick with her desire, his senses drunk on her essence. He felt her muscles clench, the spasms rippling through her and into him.

"No—yes," she said, her fingers tightening on his scalp to hold him to her.

He speared her once more as the tremors rocked through her and her back bowed, a keening sound ripping through her. Nothing had ever sounded so sweet as he covered her body with his and plunged into her.

His teeth clenched with the effort to go slow, for he felt her body shudder to adjust to his size, feared he'd hurt her. But she took control, wrapping her legs around him and arching, seating him deeper in her.

Her fingernails raked his back, his flanks, and hung on. He surrendered to her. He who never lost control with a woman did so then.

The pleasure of two bodies joined heart and soul poured through him, raging as a river, cleansing away the strictures he'd abided by all his life.

The pretense was stripped bare. Over. Ended.

Nothing could ever be more right than this moment, André thought as he held her to his side in the aftermath of the most explosive passion he'd ever felt. She was his sun and moon, his addiction.

She shifted closer and sighed. "I love you."

The avowal was a whisper of sound so hushed he nearly didn't hear it. He frowned, considering how this changed things.

This was what he'd hoped to gain—her love. But he no longer wished to crush her.

No, he had better things in store for Miss Montgomery.

He stared at her in sleep, growing more certain of his decision by the moment. It was right. It was time.

He was going to propose marriage.

CHAPTER NINE

ANDRÉ'S mobile phone chirped early the next morning. He took the call on the downstairs balcony, so as not to disturb Kira—she needed sleep, for they'd made love into the wee hours of the morning. He smiled, thinking of the passion, the feeling of rightness that hummed within him.

Hearing his detective on the line tempered his euphoria. He squinted at the horizon and wished he was upstairs with Kira, wished he'd not had to order a more thorough investigation of his lover.

"Any news on the money?" he asked, squinting at the horizon as the sun burst through the windows to gild the room in gold.

"Yes, sir. I checked my resources twice to ensure the information was correct."

The pause crackled with tension, lashing the calm André had harbored since waking with Kira curled against him. "Spit it out," he said, impatient to know the truth.

"The two million you paid to acquire the Chateau was immediately diverted into an account held by Peter Bellamy."

"You're positive?" André asked. "There can be no mistake?"

The detective answered immediately. "There's no error."

André pushed away from the railing and stormed into his suite, his gut erupting with the destructive force of a volcano, his suspicions running as hot as lava. All this time Kira's beautiful mouth had spouted lies.

She'd sworn time and again she didn't know Peter Bellamy, yet moments after receiving a wire for two million dollars the funds had been routed to Bellamy. Her protector.

What had Bellamy given Kira in return?

"There's more," the detective said.

"Concerning Miss Montgomery?"

"Yes, sir."

André laughed, the sound deceptively soft as he stared up the stairs to the bed where she still slept. "Goes from bad to worse, *oui*?"

"Not my place to say."

Of course not. That was his decision to make.

He'd used this detective before. Knew that he was like a dog with a bone, that he wouldn't give up until he'd discovered everything about the person in question. In this case, Kira.

But it had taken a damnably long time to gain the truth. André's patience for intrigue was gone. He wanted all the facts. All the secrets revealed. He wanted to see the whole picture, warts and all.

"Out with it," André said.

"I tracked down Kira Montgomery's mother," the detective said, without inflection or pause. "She swears Miss Montgomery's father is Edouard Bellamy."

The words went into André's mind and exploded, sending something dark and dangerous coursing through him. He gripped the railing as the sharp ache of betrayal speared his chest, stealing his breath. His heart skipped a beat, then started racing as the awful truth sank into his soul.

Of all the scenarios he'd imagined, of all the contrivances he'd suspected, this hadn't been one of them. This news blindsided him, drove a spike in his heart.

Oui, he'd been blind too often where Kira was concerned. Too ensnared by her beauty, her artful innocence, her passion.

Not anymore.

"There is no question this is so?" André asked.

"Only DNA tests can dispel doubts. But I spoke with the woman myself and followed up tracing the dates and places. It fits that Kira Montgomery is Edouard Bellamy's illegitimate child."

He thanked his detective and ended the communication, his mind a whirlpool of dark, putrid thoughts. Her insistence that she wasn't Peter's mistress tolled in his ears—at least in that she told the truth. *Mon Dieu*—they were brother and sister.

It was all so obvious now—Edouard Bellamy had educated her. Given her a coveted position at his La Cygne Hotel in London and forty-nine percent of Chateau Mystique. Because she was his daughter!

Mon Dieu! With Suzette dead, Edouard must have known that André would launch a takeover. But, according to the proof he had, *Peter* had sent Kira here.

She and Peter had conspired to forestall André. Not by engineering a public and humiliating end to his engagement, as he'd assumed—never mind that he and his fiancée had secretly parted ways the week before, by mutual agreement. And not by destroying a lucrative business deal that he'd worked hard to achieve.

No, she and Peter had trumped André with an innocent baby.

They'd ruthlessly plotted to force André to make a terrible choice, certain he'd choose the one that would damn him in eternal hell. For Edouard's blood coursed in his child's veins through Kira.

Kira had played well the part of corporate whore.

If André held to his vow to destroy the Bellamys he'd see the downfall of his own flesh and blood. An innocent life, caught in the crossfire.

He strode back onto the balcony and stared down at the palace he'd created. Peace eluded him.

The hell he'd been plunged into shrouded the beauty surrounding him. All he saw was Kira—memories of her loving him, challenging him, deceiving him.

His earlier thought that she'd make a good mother taunted him, enraged him. Not for *his* child.

Her conspiracy left him no choice—his only thought rested with the child. *His* child. When the baby was born, when tests had confirmed the child was his, he'd take sole custody.

Kira was a Bellamy. Not his lover, not the mother of his child, but his enemy's daughter. She was his enemy as well.

He swiped a shaky hand over his mouth, shoving compassion and his passion for her from his mind. She'd baited him—now she'd pay the price.

She'd give birth on Petit St. Marc and he'd see she had the best care money could provide. But she'd never know his child. *Never!*

He'd employ every resource available to him as he waged this war against her. When he was done with her she'd regret that she'd agreed to deceive him.

At midday, Kira went in search of André. He'd barely spoken to her on their early-morning return to Petit St. Marc, and she'd been too exhausted from their night of lovemaking to take offense. Back on the island, he'd insisted she take a nap.

She hadn't argued. But her rest had been fitful.

Keeping her secret was twisting her stomach into knots. She had to tell him now.

He was going out the door just as she descended the stairs. She quickened her steps. "Do you have a moment to talk?"

His spine stiffened, his shoulders snapping back as he stopped abruptly in the doorway. He glanced at her, and his fierce expression burned holes in her courage.

"Is it urgent?"

She thought it was vital, but, considering his mood right now, she shook her head. She'd taken the coward's way out this long. A few more hours wouldn't make any difference.

"No," she said, forcing a smile. "It can wait."

"I will see you this evening, then."

And he was gone, without any explanation of where he was taking himself off to. Not that his business was hers. Even the Chateau was his now.

Kira aimlessly strolled through the house, her mind too cluttered with worry to do anything else. She ended up at the door to André's office, surprised Otillie hadn't intercepted her yet. But the house was quiet, as if she was the only one there.

She slipped inside with thoughts of scanning his bookshelf. But the glow on his desk changed her mind. He'd not only left his computer here, but it was on.

In moments she'd accessed her mail. Her solicitor's reply slammed into her so hard she dropped on the chair.

She couldn't believe he suggested she should hire investigators to look into her claim. He insisted he'd seen the document, with her signature, authorizing the sale of her shares of the Chateau, but that he'd couldn't divulge where the money had gone.

In short, because she'd divested herself of the shares, company counsel no longer represented her.

She logged off and returned to her room, so sick at heart she could have retched. Edouard had told her Peter resented her. Told her not to contact him because he would not be receptive to her.

Had her half-brother set out to destroy her the moment their father had drawn his last breath? How could she prove it?

She was so deep into piecing together the irregular sections of this ugly puzzle that she didn't realize Otillie had entered her room until she spoke.

"You have not been drinking water, *mademoiselle*," Otillie said.

Kira glanced at her full pitcher of water and frowned. Her throat did suddenly seem parched. Her head ached from her efforts to make sense of this debacle she'd been thrust into, and she was growing more miserable.

"I forgot," she said, accepting a glass of water and drinking deeply.

"Monsieur Gauthier will not be pleased," the woman said.

That was the least of her worries, considering what she had to tell him when he returned. She sat her empty glass on the table, her spirits low, her worries shooting into the impossibly blue sky. That was when she noticed the large box on her bed.

She motioned to it. "What's that?"

"A gift for you from Monsieur Gauthier," Otillie said.

Her lips parted and her heart began racing. Two gifts in as many days? That was an extravagance she'd never experienced before.

Was this another indulgence for his kept woman? Or an apology for his earlier abruptness? Don't be a fool and look for a deeper meaning, she chided herself.

She read the attached note—*Dinner at seven. Wear this.*

No endearments. No explanations. Still she smiled as she stared at the strokes of his signature, as strong and demanding as the man.

She tore into the package, unable to stay her excitement.

The gift was a sarong, the fabric pure Carib. The soft greens, golds and browns seemed to be plucked straight from the heart of Petit St. Marc.

Kira glanced at the clock. She had less than an hour to get ready. Less than an hour before she divulged the secret that might signal an end to her idyll with André.

Forty minutes later, reality dimmed her enthusiasm. But the sarong was simply gorgeous and sexy, and she absolutely loved it.

A narrow bandeau barely covered her breasts, which were fuller, more sensitive, and flushed a telling shade of pink. Her neck and shoulders were bare, covered only by her hair, which she'd let cascade in thick curls down her back.

Three sharp raps sounded at her door. Her gaze fixed on the louvered panels, noting the tall shadow at her door.

André. He'd come for her.

She tamped down the nervous laugh that threatened to bubble up in her. This was a wretched time to be struck by a case of anxiety.

Taking deep breaths did nothing to calm her. Her hands shook as she smoothed her palms down her skirt, her stomach heaved—muscles clutching. Her legs trembled, as if ready to give way.

She forced herself to walk slowly toward the door, even managed to affect a welcoming smile as she opened the louvers.

The sight of him robbed her of breath. He was dressed entirely in black. The silky shirt lay open at his neck, exposing whirls of thick black hair.

The long sleeves were ruched up, yet full, lending him a rogue's look. The trousers lay flat over his washboard belly and hugged the long muscular lines of his legs.

Casual elegance, she thought.

His face was a study in art itself, the brow strong, the nose straight and not too thin.

His cheekbones were high, the jaw was firm and dusted with a rakish five o'clock shadow, making him look more daring. More resolute. More sexy. Her pirate.

"Bonsoir." His sculpted lips pulled into a smile that melted her heart. "You are beautiful."

"So are you," she said, her heart brimming with love.

She'd never been so terrified in her life, but they'd get past this last obstacle. They had to. Love would find a way.

"Thank you for the sarong. It's fabulous."

"It suits you."

His dark gaze swept over her, much like a predator would watch easy prey. Sudden tension needled up her limbs, and she had the sudden urge to flee. Run while she had the chance.

Then he extended his arm to her, smiled that pirate's grin, and the moment was gone. "Shall we?"

Kira nodded and slipped her arm in the crook of his. The heat and power under her hand left her breathless, even more unsure of herself.

She'd been affected by his potent sensuality from the first time she'd met him, but what she sensed in him now had nothing to do with carnal promises.

The leashed anger in him was palpable, stripping away her

shaky confidence and flooding her with renewed apprehension. She'd felt that same raging tension in him when he'd come to the Chateau, when he'd forced her to leave with him.

"What's wrong, André?"

"Nothing. All is in order."

Yet a litany of doom pulsed in the air as she descended the stairs. He walked indecently close behind her, his hand on the small of her back, one finger resting in a dimple on her derrière.

The heat of him burned her through her dress, branding her skin. But the touch blazed with power rather than affection.

He seated her at a table dressed in stark white, and she finally filled her lungs with air when he strode to his chair. Crystal chandeliers held long white tapers, their golden flames casting a sultry aura over the table.

He poured sparkling water for her, champagne for himself. The romance of it wasn't lost on her. But there was no warmth in his eyes.

She took a sip of water and her stomach pitched, rebelling again. She would not be able to manage food tonight. She'd not be able to tolerate this tension that made her head spin.

A bead of sweat popped out on her temple, slowly streaking down her face. She dabbed at it with what she hoped was an offhand movement, hating that her hand shook, that his dark, expressionless eyes remained on her. Inquisitive. Or inquisitional?

Was this how a mouse felt when cornered by a cat? Her stomach fluttered and her breath came short and shallow.

Sweat gathered beneath her breasts. She licked lips that had gone dry. How could she possibly confess her secret when he was in this dark, dangerous mood?

This moment was more unsettling than when he'd swept into the Chateau and forced her to leave with him. The eloquent hands that had brought her such pleasure held his glass too tightly. His admirable posture was too rigid, the broad shoulders held with military precision, his spine too unbending.

He'd hated her then because he'd believed she was Peter's

mistress. The truth would be worse. She knew it. No matter that they'd shared exquisite passion in each other's arms. No matter that she carried his child. No matter that she had somehow fallen in love with him.

Her heart broke as she met his dark gaze. He was still the most handsome man she'd ever met, and she was painfully aware this could be the last time she shared anything but disdain with him. However could she begin?

"I used your computer today," she said, to break the horrid silence that roared in the room.

He took a sip of champagne and regarded her over the lavish tulip glass with eyes that caught the light and threw its glare back at her. Like an inquisitor. Reserved. Controlling.

"Did you email your brother again?" he asked.

Kira nearly lost her grip on her glass—did lose her breath. He knew. My God, he already knew her secret! No wonder he stared at her so coldly.

"No." She set her glass down with care, her hand shaking so badly it took effort. She drew in a breath, then another, but neither seemed enough for her starving lungs. "I never have."

He snorted and tossed back his drink. When he looked at her this time, his gaze was openly hostile.

A demoralizing dread seeped into her.

His rage threatened to consume her. Burn her alive. The flames different than the passion, more powerful because of the dark emotion fueling the fire. This inferno would not just burn her. It would kill her.

"How long have you known?" she asked, proud her voice remained calm despite the tempest whirling around her.

"Since this morning." He set his flute down and reached for the champagne bottle, his movements slow, precise.

He poured champagne in his glass, his finesse obviously shaken for he spilled some on the table. His scowl conveyed his annoyance at the minuscule lack of control.

She stared at the bubbles in his glass and thought ironically that they mirrored the riot going on in her stomach—a cold boil that popped around her, leaving her on shaky ground.

Kira chanced a look at him and wished she hadn't, for his rage was evident in the hard, unyielding lines of his face. She stared at her hands, the fingers bleached white from gripping the table linen as the awful truth weighed her down.

She'd never been subjected to such cold scrutiny. Never been the recipient of such scathing wrath.

Never wanted to right a wrong more than she did at this moment. "I—I intended to tell you tonight, after dinner."

His laugh was brittle and cold. "But of course you would say that now."

"It's the truth. I've thought of little else today."

Except for those moments when she'd become lost in the memory of lying in André's arms. Of those strong hands playing over her skin, making her senses sing with pleasure.

"Interesting, as your deceit has been on my mind as well," he said, his thumb idly stroking the tulip glass.

She looked at those hands now, watching that slow glide, and flushed hot as her breasts grew heavier. She couldn't still want him to touch her, to pleasure her? Yet she knew if he did she'd be lost in his arms again.

Panic took root in her, for her body was betraying her. Her body wanted him any way she could get him. She was weak—exhausted by his relentless onslaught of her senses.

She hated his power over her. Hated that he was playing the tyrant to perfection.

That would stop now. She wasn't afraid of him. She was his equal—his lover—whether he admitted it or not.

"If you'd just allow me to explain?"

He made a magnanimous gesture with his hand, the shadow of his movement caressing the wall much like that same hand had caressed her last night. "Please do."

Kira took another sip of water, hating that her hand trembled, that her breathing hitched, that her stomach remained queasy. She could barely force the much needed fluid down her throat, even though she was thirsty. It had been like that all day—nerves and tension and the unknown, all battling together in a gigantic knot within her.

"You must understand," she began. "I—I've never told anyone before, you see. Edouard insisted, and I never thought to disobey."

"Then I should feel honored to be the first to hear your story." He saluted her with his glass and drank deeply. "Bravo to you and your father for launching this honeytrap. You planned it well—right down to getting pregnant."

"There was no conspiracy," she said. "I just came here to meet with you about the Chateau. How dare you insinuate that I set out to trap you?"

He smirked, the expression a barbed taunt that angered her more than any insult, any accusation. "How fitting that you should begin with a lie."

She closed her eyes a moment, knowing he'd read it as guilt but no longer caring, knowing he'd not listen to her denials again. He'd believe what he wished.

He'd close his mind to the truth.

The door to the kitchen opened, and a Carib bustled in to serve them. Kira stared at the exquisite meal and knew that she'd never get a morsel down her throat.

She draped her napkin over the plate, hating that she'd offend the cook, and met André's hooded glare. She read hatred in his eyes. All targeted at her.

"It is senseless to continue. You know the truth and you've condemned me without hearing my side. Enjoy your meal." She rose, praying her trembling legs would support her.

"Sit down." His command cracked like a whip.

She hesitated a moment, staring into his dark eyes and silently challenging him. A crazy thing to do, for she knew André could pounce on her with the stealth and power of a jaguar.

He could crush her with a condemning look, rip her heart out with a word—for he'd done both with ease. Was doing so now. And the pain of his hatred was tearing her apart inside.

She grabbed the edge of the table, her fingernails biting into the polished surface. "If you'll listen to me, I'll stay."

He leaned forward in his chair, his gaze never leaving hers, his anger so strong she felt it pulsing in the room, in her veins. "You'll stay whether I choose to listen or not."

"Fine. Rant and pound your chest if you like." She dropped onto the chair, so defeated, so weary. "How did you find out?"

He pushed his own food away without sampling it and lounged back in his chair with an insolent air. "Through a private detective. He tracked down your mother."

Kira stared at him, unblinking, an incredulous laugh escaping her. How ironic that the one person she hadn't seen in over twenty years should return to ruin her life.

"She's still alive, then?" she said, hearing the bitterness ring in her voice and not caring.

She'd given up being concerned about the woman who'd given birth to her long ago.

"You don't like her?" he said.

She shrugged. "I told you before, I barely remember her."

He looked away, frowning, and she wondered what went through his mind. He'd had a mother and father who'd loved him. A family that cared.

"I hope you didn't pay her for the information," she said, angry. Hurt. "She made far too much off me years ago."

"Did she?"

"Yes. She sold me to my father—which was odd, since he didn't want me either."

Something shifted in his eyes, a flicker of something warm. Or was it just a reflection from the candles?

Kira didn't know anymore. Her head pounded and her back ached. She hurt inside. Felt drained, battered. Everything was an effort. Sitting here, talking, breathing, thinking about what had happened. Worrying about what was to come.

"Tell me," he said.

She shook her head, believing there was no point in divulging so much now. All her life she'd held her secrets close, hid them and hid the pain.

"Tell me, *ma chérie*," he said, his voice softer, lower, intimate.

How devastating that the hushed timbre of his voicing the endearment melted the starch holding her up. She dashed away a tear that slipped free, but another quickly formed, then too many to stop.

Silly, really, for she couldn't remember crying for her mother. Not once.

"I was an accident. She never wanted me, but for some reason she kept me for a few years. Until I was hurt in a boating mishap." She frowned, remembering that horrid event so clearly, yet she had trouble remembering her mother's face. "Edouard told me that she offered me to him then. He paid her price and I never saw her again."

"How old were you?"

"Nearly five."

"That's when he placed you in an elite boarding school in England?"

"Yes. I spent the rest of my formative years being shuffled from nannies to boarding school. Not once did my father welcome me to his home for a holiday or a brief visit. Not once."

She looked away, for there was really nothing more to tell. She had studied, read, and had seen Edouard once or twice a year when the mood had struck him.

And all the while she'd dreamed of one day having a family. Of having someone in her life who cared about her. Who would love her and who she could love in return.

Her hand stole to her belly to cradle her baby. She would have that dream become a reality soon.

"What was your reward for seducing me?" André asked.

She shook her head, scowling, angry that he thought she'd seduce him for money, that he equated her with her mother. "There was no reward, because there was no conspiracy."

"The truth, *s'il vous plaît*."

She slapped both palms on the table, her patience and energy spent. "I am telling you the truth."

He swore and jumped to his feet, chest heaving, fists clenched tight. His gaze raked over her, furious, insulting in its curt, deliberate movement.

Then he stalked from the room.

Kira put her head down and sighed, giving in to the tremors that whispered over her. But that only made her dizziness worse and set her stomach churning. If she could just find the strength to return to her room…

She heard heavy footsteps approaching. She'd tarried too long. Her respite was gone.

André stopped beside her chair, currents of anger radiating from his body in hot, scalding waves. He dropped a stack of paper before her.

"Try to deny these."

She stared at the heading, recognizing her corporate email address. Above it was an address she was unfamiliar with.

She skimmed the first note and paled. Then read another. And another.

This couldn't be…

But it was.

This was the electronic proof he'd told her about. The evidence that she and Peter Bellamy had conspired to launch a smear campaign against André. Sickening details of every calculated move, right down to her agreeing to come here on the pretext of a meeting when her intent was to seduce André while Peter alerted the paparazzi.

Except she *hadn't* carried on this dialogue with Peter. She *hadn't* set out to seduce André and humiliate him publicly, so the large corporation he'd been trying to solidify a deal with would pull out because he lacked family values. And she certainly hadn't tried to become pregnant.

She hadn't been aware of Peter's calculating plans until now. Hadn't written one word of this correspondence. But it had been sent from her email address, using her electronic signature. How could she prove she'd had no part in this? She couldn't.

Still, she lifted her chin and said simply, "I didn't write any of these."

CHAPTER TEN

ANDRÉ had expected her denial. But when the lie spilled from her sweet mouth the cynical curl to his lips eased a fraction. His blood slowed, his chest growing warm, his heart hesitating. For he almost believed her. Almost.

His weakness for her disgusted him.

Kira stood up and took a step toward him, stopped, her throat working, her face as white and delicate as the lace tablecloth. Her gaze lifted to his, her expression open, vulnerable.

He fisted his hands at his sides, fighting the impulse to reach for her, pull her close. Kiss her. Caress her. Sweep the servings from the table and take her here. Now.

Tell her all would be fine. Tell her that he forgave her.

That he loved her.

He'd vowed never to say those words. He'd thought it a simple promise to keep, for he believed himself incapable of such a crippling, all-consuming emotion.

"Someone else wrote these emails," she said.

He laughed, thinking that for someone possessing such guile she was quite naïve. "Using *your* email server? *Your* electronic signature?"

"Someone hacked into my account," she said, and frowned, clearly troubled, her clasped hands trembling.

Guilt, pure and simple. He'd trapped her in her own lie, and she was afraid. Terrified of what he'd do.

For once he was uncertain how to proceed. The satisfaction that usually filled him over besting an enemy was absent. Because in hurting her he hurt his child. He couldn't abide that.

Mon Dieu, but he hated this untenable situation, hated the desire for her that wouldn't die. He drove his fingers through his hair, tugging the strands, when he really wanted to weave his fingers in *her* hair, feel the skeins of silk brush his bare chest, his thighs.

Madness. He'd lost his mind. Lost his heart.

Lost *her* since she persisted in lying to him.

"Only one person had access to your account. You." He nodded to the emails lying on the table. "Admit it, *ma chérie*. Be done with the lies."

She shook her head slowly, fat tears spilling from her eyes. His gut tightened as he watched them course down her ashen face, and he jammed his hands in his pockets to keep from reaching out and wiping them from her soft cheeks.

He'd done it. Broken the enemy. Bested her. Won the game. But his victory was hollow.

He hurt more than she possibly could, because she'd forced him to take a resolute stand. He wouldn't forsake honor. He couldn't forget his vow of vengeance.

She drew in a shuddering breath, her slender shoulders squaring, her chin lifting even though it trembled. Proud. Strong. Qualities he admired in her.

"Could you have ever loved me?" she asked, the raw quality in her voice belying her courage.

"The daughter of my enemy? Never," he said.

She flinched, as if he'd bellowed the denial, as if he'd slapped her. As if she believed him that easily. "Then let me go, André. Let *us* go. For if you can't set aside your hatred for me, you won't be able to for our child either."

He stared at her, incredulous. Never mind that the same realization had crossed his mind. He couldn't live with her, and he wasn't sure he could live without her.

"One has nothing to do with the other."

"You're wrong. Can you honestly say it doesn't bother you that your child is part Bellamy?"

Her question was a knife-thrust to his heart. His own nagging doubts the twist that filleted the emotions he'd held in check for so long. He crossed to the French doors that opened onto the rear terrace, staring at his meticulously groomed garden, whose wild fragrance paled in comparison to the subtle scent that was uniquely Kira.

Her fragrance reached out to him with silken arms, commanding all his senses, promising pleasure. Promising hope.

It would be so easy to put pleasure before honor. Go to her. Love her. Forget the world for this night. But their differences would still be there in the morning.

One shallow breath drew her deeper into his blood, into his soul, into his heart. When he'd brought her here he'd foolishly believed he could use her and then cast her aside. Forget her.

He couldn't. Not then. Certainly not after he'd discovered she was with child. And not now, when his own emotions were so raw.

But he couldn't forgive either. Forgiveness wasn't in his blood. And she'd deceived him in the worst possible way.

André loved passionately, and he hated with the same intensity. There were no gray areas. No subtle riffling of the emotions at either extreme.

So he loved Kira and he hated her. The two emotions were ripping him apart.

"Let me go," she said again, more strident this time.

Never, he thought, pressing a palm to the cool dark wood, feeling the grain bite into his flesh. He couldn't bear to let her leave, and he couldn't stand to live with a Bellamy.

"Where would you go?" he asked, turning to face her, hiding his own inner war behind practiced insouciance. "To Peter?"

She looked away, eyes closed, as if the sight of him pained her. Good. She should hurt as much as he hurt. Should feel this awful ache to her soul. For she'd come to him first, seduced him, bound him to her forever through their child.

"To the Chateau. Please, let me return to my job."

"Out of the question." He had to protect his child from the Bellamys, and the only way he could do that was by keeping her here, where he could watch her, or at least have her watched. "Your only job for the next six months is pampering yourself and my baby."

"I don't need to be pampered," she said, her eyes too wide. Too bright. "I'll fight you every day that you keep me on the island against my will."

He smiled grimly, for there'd be no winner in this battle. "I expect no less from a Bellamy."

Kira gripped the table, barely able to breathe through her choking anguish. The headache that had plagued her all day pounded relentlessly, each drubbing in her veins taunting her challenge to André.

He hadn't moved. Hadn't so much as blinked. Just watched her with a lethal intensity that sucked the moisture from her mouth. She licked her lips, but they burned, the skin too dry.

Her throat felt parched. She reached for her glass, but her hand shook so badly she tipped it over.

"Leave it," he said, when she attempted to mop up the mess she'd made.

She ran her tongue over her lips again—so very thirsty, so very tired. The carafe of water was so far from her. The room spun. Her world careened out of control.

Kira had to get out of here—away from him and his heated glare. She couldn't fight him now. Not with her strength depleted, with her heart breaking in two.

She took a shaky breath, steadied herself, and stared at the intricately carved newel posts, hoping if she focused on the staircase the dizziness would be tolerable.

"Where are you going?" he asked, grabbing her arm to stop her from walking past him.

"Let me go."

His grip eased a fraction. "Answer me."

She closed her eyes, disgusted her body ached to lean into him. "To my room."

"You haven't eaten."

She glared at him. "I lost my appetite."

His seductive lips flattened in a disagreeable line. "You need to eat. I'll send Otillie up with a tray."

"Don't bother. I won't be able to keep anything down tonight."

He dropped his hand, only to punish her more by placing both hands on her shoulders. "You need food. The baby—"

"How dare you think of my child's welfare now?" She shoved away from him and headed toward the stairs, each step a challenge.

Odd twinges ribboned across her belly. Her back ached so badly she thought it would break in two.

She reached the stairs and grabbed the newel post, clinging to it for balance and drawing air into her lungs. But each breath only fanned the flames that felt like they were burning out of control within her heart, her soul.

"My child. *Mon enfant, ma chérie*. Don't forget that."

As if she could. She looked back at him, thinking he was still the most handsome man she'd ever met. And dangerous, leaning a hip against the table, a replenished champagne flute held casually in one elegant hand.

"Go to hell, André." She started up the stairs, each step slow, unsteady, her head throbbing, her vision blurring.

"I am already there," he said, his voice sounding oddly distant.

They both were, she thought.

She made it to the third step when cramps sliced through her, far worse than the last time.

The doctor's admonition blared in her mind. Avoid the sun. Drink two liters of water a day.

She hadn't done either. But she would drink her fill as soon as she reached her room. As soon as she was away from André and his dark accusations.

Her next step sent pain knifing across her middle, so sharp and piercing it took her breath away. She gasped and bent double, gripping the railing for dear life and cradling her belly with the other. But her world continued to spin away.

"André!"

She heard glass shatter. Then he was beside her, gathering her in his arms, his face ashen beneath his tan. But it was the stricken look in his eyes that terrified her, for it confirmed her worst fear.

"Our baby," she got out, as black pinpricks danced before her eyes to block out the light.

She fell into the blackness, into his arms. Her last tormenting thought was that she was losing the baby.

André paced the hospital corridor. The last hour had passed in a hellish nightmare, from the time Kira had collapsed in his arms until they'd arrived on Martinique. He'd never felt so helpless, so afraid for anyone in his life. He'd never been gripped with such crushing guilt—even after his parents' deaths.

For all his tough exterior and his vows to keep his heart removed from a woman, André wept silent tears in the velvety night, holding her close to his heart, his chest so tight he could barely breathe.

Seeing Kira so helpless had stripped him of all pretense, all thought but moving heaven and earth to save her and his baby's life. But as they'd raced across a moonlit sea fear had clung to him like the dense sea mist.

She'd been too pale, too cold. She hadn't roused, hadn't done anything but lie in his arms like a rag doll.

He hadn't prayed in ages, but he had then, and he continued to now, in the hospital. Prayed and paced. He relived every tension-riddled moment between him and Kira that had led up to her collapse. He held himself to blame.

Mon Dieu, he should have recognized something was wrong with her at dinner. But he'd been too intent on castigating her for being a Bellamy, for trying to ruin him, staunchly clinging to his pride, his vengeance.

He'd attacked her with the same energy and ruthless bent as he would a corporate adversary. Perhaps worse, because his emotions were tangled in knots when it came to Kira.

For once in his life he couldn't separate his business and personal life. She was too much a part of both. He'd removed her from her job and placed her into the role of his mistress.

But she didn't fit that image well because she was carrying his child.

A child whose life he'd endangered. A child who might die. *Sacre bleu!* If anything happened to either of them he'd never forgive himself. Never!

The accusations he'd hurled at her played over and over in his mind. She denied authoring those emails. Still denied she'd conferred with Peter Bellamy.

Yet the small fortune he'd paid for her shares had gone straight to Peter. He'd been sure she'd contact her half-brother when she was offered the chance on St. Barth. But, no, she'd emailed her solicitor, believing that ineffectual man could somehow help her regain her shares. He'd offered no solution. In fact he'd seemed pleased she was no longer a part of the "family" corporation. Had she been disowned? Betrayed?

It seemed that way. Peter had never contacted André after he'd seen him shuffle Kira from the Chateau. It was as if Peter had been glad to see her go. But if that were true, why had her millions gone to Bellamy? And why send the paparazzi to the island again?

The doctor emerged from the emergency room, his white coat fluttering wide. But it was his scowl that captured André's attention.

"Monsieur Gauthier. On your word, you promised that Miss Montgomery would heed my advice, no?"

"*Oui*, I did." But it was obvious he'd failed miserably. He'd been too intent on his quest for vengeance to care for the mother of his child. "How is she—and my baby?"

"Miss Montgomery is seriously dehydrated. We could not rouse her enough to drink fluids." The doctor paused and shook his head, and André's gut clenched. He was fearing the worst, fearing he'd lost them both. "We've forced fluids into her intravenously, and she is improving now."

"The baby?" he asked, afraid to hope they'd avoided a heart-wrenching disaster.

The doctor smiled. "The fetus has a strong heartbeat."

André simply stared at him, for though he'd believed Kira carried a child, he'd never thought a heartbeat could be detected so soon. He'd not thought of anything but vengeance and lust in turn.

"I ordered tests to check her chemical balance. If her electrolytes are normal, we will release her today."

"No!" André ran a hand through his hair, damning the way it shook.

The doctor canted his head to the side. "No?"

"She can't be trusted to hydrate herself this soon," André said, hoping the doctor wouldn't see through that flimsy excuse.

In truth, he didn't trust himself around Kira right now, for his emotions were still bouncing between love and hate.

The doctor rubbed his chin and frowned. "She will not like being detained, *monsieur*, for she has told me she wants to go home."

Home. The Chateau Mystique had been her home, and he'd taken that from her. He'd stripped her of everything.

"You will be rewarded for keeping her here for a few days," André said, calculating that would give him enough time to do what he must. "Tell her she must stay, for the baby's welfare."

"Very well, *monsieur*. We appreciate your largesse." The doctor turned to leave, then paused. "You may see her now."

André wanted to, but he didn't dare see her face to face until he found out if she'd been telling him the truth. Because if she was innocent, as she proclaimed, then his honor demanded that he right the wrongs he'd done her.

But even if that wasn't the case he would give her anything and do everything to keep her well, so she would deliver a healthy child. *Their* child.

His chest tightened, his heart heavy and burning. Raw.

He'd been ready to marry her. To make her his forever.

But she was a Bellamy, and no matter how much André desired her, no matter how much his heart ached to make her his, he couldn't marry his enemy's daughter.

Kira sat in bed, staring out the window at the thin white clouds drifting across the azure sky. The scene hadn't changed much in the two days she'd been hospitalized. Clear blue sky broken by occasional clouds, their formation the only variance.

Inside nothing changed either. The same nurse and doctor tended to her every whim, as if she were royalty. The food was above par, though her appetite was nil. But she ate and drank for the baby's sake.

Thank God her child was safe. If she'd lost the baby, or hurt it in any way because of her neglect, she never would have forgiven herself.

But she'd lost André. She was sure of it, for she hadn't heard from him since that confrontational scene at his house.

She'd relived that moment when she had walked away from him a thousand times. The anger blazing in his eyes had burned into her, incinerating her will to win his heart, her determination to carve a niche for herself and their child in his life.

Yet she was tormented by that moment when she'd collapsed, when she'd seen pain and regret and fear in his eyes.

Tears blurred her vision and she angrily swiped them away. He hadn't visited her at the hospital once. How could he abandon her and the baby? How could he just walk away?

Because she was Edouard Bellamy's daughter.

He hated her—he hated their child as well.

A hollow ache expanded in her chest, her heart grieving for what would never be.

She should be thankful the ugly truth was revealed. That he'd left her in peace. That she'd likely never see him again. For if she did it would be a tense, unpleasant meeting.

She should be happy. But she'd never been so heartbroken.

On the morning of the third day something roused her from a restless sleep, snapping her awake and wary. Kira scanned her room, her heart accelerating as her gaze fell on the tall man standing at the window, his back to her.

She stared at those incredibly broad shoulders and blinked. Was she dreaming?

No. This was real. André had come at last, and her foolish heart was rejoicing even as her brain tried to warn her to move with caution around him.

Everything about him pulsed with raw intensity—his potent masculinity, his arrogant bearing, his brooding indifference, all more sharply defined as he stared out the window.

"How long have you been here?" she asked.

"Not long. The doctor says you and the baby are well."

"We were lucky," she said, detecting no rancor in his voice.

But there was no emotion either. Or rather no more than one might bestow on a stranger in the wake of an accident. Simply a comment in the face of a near tragedy—an acknowledgement of survival—something to fill the tense silence.

She sighed, unable to be that detached even now. "Thank you for getting us here so quickly."

One shoulder lifted in a careless shrug. "Don't. I should never have confronted you with such—" He waved a hand, as if trying to snatch a word from thin air, as if annoyed that he couldn't grasp a title for their situation.

"Animosity?" she supplied.

"Venom," he said. "My behavior was inexcusable."

"Yes," she said, unwilling to forgive him so easily for setting her up for a verbal attack from which she couldn't defend herself, unwilling to forgive them both for not putting their child's needs first.

It would not happen again. No matter what he said. No matter what happened in the future. *If* they had a future. At this moment she could not guess what was going through André's mind.

"We have unfinished business between us," he said.

"Business? Are you talking about the Chateau?"

"No, personal business."

Surely he didn't mean—? "We have a child between us."

"I am aware of my obligations, *ma chérie*."

She flinched, angry and hurt that he chose to regard the tiny life they'd created as an obligation. Hurt that he thought so little of their precious child, and angry at herself for deluding herself about André Gauthier.

He didn't want her, and he certainly didn't want their child. He was just like her father—cold, calculating, ruthless.

André had returned for one reason—to bestow a settlement on her. To shuffle her out of his life. He'd likely want her to sign a document agreeing to his denouncing any obligation to her or their child.

"Fine. State your business," she said, her fingers bunching the sheet in a tight knot that rivaled the hard ache in her stomach.

"I have confronted Peter Bellamy."

She released a bitter laugh, more saddened than surprised that André still believed the worst of her. "Did he deny there was a conspiracy? Or did he perhaps swear I'd concocted some devilish scheme alone?"

"Neither. Peter laughed, pleased by the turmoil he'd wrought. He hates you."

She'd known her half-brother resented her. She'd deduced he'd been the one who set out to ruin her. But she'd not considered that he'd be so pleased by her downfall. That he hated her so much.

Her insides felt raw, scraped of emotion, of feeling. She'd been a fool, longing for family, doing as asked by her mother for that brief time she'd known her, and by her father, who had been little more than a name throughout her life. She'd not asked for more, for it had been drummed into her that what she had was all she'd get.

She'd abided by her father's rules, and in the end her family had betrayed her. Family she hadn't even known.

But it crushed her spirit, her heart, that André had shut her out of his life after all they'd shared. Even now he stared out the window, as if unable to tolerate looking at her.

"Yet you still believe the worst of me," she said.

His shoulders snapped a bit straighter. "You were innocent of his machinations."

That admission failed to tell her how he felt about her, only that he believed her claim of innocence long after the fact.

"Is that the business you came here to attend to, then?" she asked.

"Not entirely." André strode toward her, his broad shoulders straight, his jaw resolute, his arrogantly handsome face—

"My God!" She leaned forward, her heart hammering as she took in the bruises, the cut lip, the swollen eye. "What happened to you?"

His fierce scowl made him look more ravaged, more dangerous, despite the custom-tailored suit that screamed sophistication. "Peter and I fought as our ancestors did when pirating ships collided."

Her mouth dropped open. She was shocked that the billionaire who was famed for his rapier-sharp verbal sparring had engaged in a physical fight on her behalf. That he seemed proud of it. What was she to make of that?

"You attacked him?"

"*Oui*. I could have killed him for his underhand dealings involving you, but I didn't," he said, looking away from her as if the admission pained him.

A tiny bud of hope unfurled inside her. He'd stood up for her. But that didn't mean he cared for her.

André was a complicated man. His reasons for fighting Peter

could have nothing to do with her at all. It could all center around defending his honor.

"Why, André? Why did you do it?"

He jammed his hands in his trouser pockets and stared down on her, his bearing so rigid she felt it snap the air with electricity like an approaching thunderstorm. "I have no tolerance for a man who endeavors to ruin his sister."

"Illegitimate half-sister," she said, unable to feel anything but pity for the half-brother who'd attacked her with such hatred.

"The same Bellamy blood flows in you and in him."

She laughed at that, for even her father hadn't welcomed her into his legitimate family. He'd sequestered her from them all her life, and made it clear she was never to admit her paternity to anyone. He'd stressed that if she ever directly contacted his family there'd be severe consequences to bear.

She'd abided by his wishes because she'd learned to be happy on her own. Because she'd had no wish to cause more scandal. Yet Peter obviously hadn't felt the same.

"In this case water is thicker than blood," she said.

He stared at her a long, uncomfortable moment. "*Oui*. You became the target of familial vengeance the day Edouard placed you in a position of power at Le Cygne."

She suspected it had begun the day Peter had learned about her existence, but he'd bided his time until Edouard couldn't defend her. "Peter obviously resented that his father had acknowledged his by-blow so richly."

"*Oui*. But it was your solicitor who took umbrage."

Had she heard him correctly? "Claude? But why?"

"You really don't know?" He faced her, and she shook her head in answer. "Claude Deveaux is Edouard's brother-in-law."

More family. More hatred. She blinked back angry tears, sick of being manipulated by powerful men with hidden agendas.

"I trusted him," she said.

"You made it easy for them both."

She reached for her glass of water and drank, waiting for

him to expound, forcing more than a sip down her emotion-clogged throat. But he simply watched her, his expression unreadable.

"How long have you known all this?" she asked.

He shrugged, a careless gesture she loathed and loved in turn, for she was never sure if he was the uncaring rake or the troubled man she'd lost her heart to. "I suspected something was amiss when your shares went public. But I didn't begin to believe you were a pawn until our jaunt to St. Barthélemy, when you emailed your solicitor demanding answers."

When had he had the time to check his computer? Or had he charged someone else to search it?

The Windward Islands were his domain. His world. She was merely a puppet in it, dancing to the melody he'd arranged.

"You set me up—knowing I was desperate to get word out," she said.

That emotionless mask she detested stared back at her, giving nothing away. "I was certain you'd contact Peter, that I'd catch you devising a new plot to ruin me. But you didn't."

She called herself a fool for not suspecting the trap. For trusting him. *Trust.* As he'd said, she had made it easy for his enemies—and him—to deceive her.

Her chin came up, and she damned its tremor. "You knew that I didn't email Peter, yet you still believed I'd conspired with him?"

He shrugged. "You are a Bellamy."

"And you could never trust a Bellamy. You certainly could never love one." Not her. Not even their child.

His jaw clenched so tight she feared he'd crack the bone, but his eyes gave nothing away. "I will provide for you. Nothing more."

Kira set her glass down carefully, when her anger goaded her to lob the whole thing at him. That night on St. Barth, when he'd held her close to his heart and called her his love, his darling, she'd believed him. She'd thought that they would have a chance for a lifetime of happiness in each other's arms.

She'd hoped they could surmount any obstacle, though she'd known it wouldn't be easy for him to accept her parentage.

She hadn't totally given up hope. She'd foolishly trusted that love would conquer all.

But in the morning he'd treated her with biting indifference, as if he was furious with her again, and she'd feared the wondrous night had been a dream.

She'd never guessed it was because he'd discovered she was Edouard's daughter. That he'd intended to lay a trap for her on Petit St. Marc instead of coming to her and talking it out.

Something in her changed, twisted, died. He'd used her so well—in bed and out. Would continue doing so if she let him.

And, sadly, she wanted him with every breath she took. Her weakness toward him shamed her.

Unabashedly, Kira knew she'd never meet another man she loved with the same intensity as she did André. She'd never even try, for she'd never trust another man that much again.

It wasn't worth the heartache.

She'd found her one great love. And she'd lost him.

"Do you feel *any* guilt for your part in this?" she asked, her voice cracking as she felt the rift between them grow wider.

"I did what I had to."

And so would she. She'd take the only course left to her.

The men in her life had used her. None of them had cared for her, respected her. Not her father, who'd seen her as an obligation. Not her half-brother or his uncle, who viewed her as a usurper they must eliminate at all costs. And certainly not André, who'd used her in the worst way, by capturing her heart completely just to satisfy his quest for vengeance.

"I hope Peter's face looks as battered as yours. I hope you're both in pain." She stared at his beautifully masculine features, her tears unable to put out her fiery heartache. "I hope never to see you again."

His body jolted, so slightly she'd have missed it if she

hadn't been staring at him. Or maybe it was just a mirage caused by her tears.

She'd meant to shock him. But she'd shocked herself as well. For her love for this man was so great that she already grieved over having André in her life.

"Is that your wish?" he asked.

She forced the lie past her dry lips. "Yes. It's the only way. For you have no room in your heart for a Bellamy."

A muscle in his cheek throbbed to the wild beat of her heart as he pulled an envelope from his jacket pocket and dropped it on the foot of the bed. The battering to his pride was evident in his bleak gaze that touched hers briefly, like a fleeting kiss, bittersweet.

"Au revoir, mon amour."

He walked from her room, and she bit her tongue to keep from calling him back. Her breath hitched, her tears fell in a scalding waterfall, but they couldn't wash away the hurt.

This pain was too great to ignore. She needed time to deal with all that had happened—time to heal, time to sort it out in her mind. She had to search her heart for what she should do.

So in the quiet of her room she curled into a ball and cried for her loss. And thanked God that through her child she'd always be tied to André. She'd always have a part of him to love.

Long hours later, Kira opened the envelope with trembling fingers, suspecting André had made provision for her as he would a mistress. She wouldn't take it, of course. For that would sully the love they'd had.

She unfolded the paper and read, the chill that had gripped her fading as she read the document. Once. Twice.

Her gaze fell on the accompanying bank draft and her heart raced. She could scarce draw a decent breath as the enormity of what he'd done sank in.

All the shares of Chateau Mystique had been transferred to her. The hotel was solely hers—as was the bank draft for four million dollars. A fortune. All hers.

She'd gotten more than she'd wanted—would never have to depend on a man's charity or whim again. But without André in her life having it all meant nothing.

CHAPTER ELEVEN

KIRA had been back at the Chateau for an entire month—enough time to reevaluate her staff and replace those untrustworthy sorts. The number was few, and those who had stayed exhibited the loyalty she'd always hoped to inspire.

Work filled her days, and the wonder of going into her second trimester warmed her lonely nights.

But her heart bled for André, for the loss of what they'd held in their grasp and for the crippling pain of letting it go. She'd been too afraid of following in her mother's footsteps to fight harder for their love. For believing that they could surmount any odds.

So she dreamed he'd stride into the Chateau as before, and take her back to his island. As days turned into weeks, she knew that wasn't going to happen.

André wasn't coming back to her—and why should he?

She was a Bellamy. She'd told him she never wanted to see him again.

He'd taken her words to heart—words she'd spoken in anger, words she wished she could call back.

Anger boiled in Kira like a storm-tossed sea. She couldn't accept that he wanted nothing to do with the innocent life they'd created. Wouldn't believe it—not until he told her so.

And if that were the case… Then she'd love her child enough for both of them.

Kira smiled and pressed a hand on the tiny bulge of her belly.

For the first time today she'd felt a fluttering there, the wings of an angelic butterfly making itself known.

Her baby.

Hers and André's.

It pained her to think that his hatred had poisoned him so, that it had killed their love.

But he'd never said he loved her. Never said he wanted her in his life. Even if he had told her in so many words that he would fight for what he wanted.

He didn't want her.

Maybe for him it had just been lust. What else explained how he had cut her and their child from his life?

He'd had his revenge, his say.

But she hadn't. She wanted closure.

And she desperately wanted to see him, touch him, kiss him. She loved him. That would never change.

She pinched her eyes shut, almost feeling his touch, his scent, his potent power sweeping her away.

Yes, she wanted André. Ached for him still.

Countless nights she'd picked up the phone, then talked herself out of ringing him. She wouldn't chase after him. She wouldn't grovel and beg, no matter how much she ached for him. But she had to talk to him once more. Just once.

So that night she put the call through. But Otillie answered, because André wasn't in residence. He was miserable, the older woman claimed, and begged her to come back.

"*Monsieur*—he does not eat. Does not sleep," Otillie said.

Kira gripped the phone tighter, torn over what she wanted to do and what she had vowed not to do. "I don't know—"

"Please, Mademoiselle Montgomery. Come home."

Home. How odd that she'd begun to think of the island as just that. She pinched her eyes shut again, debating whether to listen to her head or her heart.

Her baby made the decision for her, giving her the tiny kick she needed.

"Expect me in a few days," she said.

Kira brimmed with excitement as she dashed to the pharmacy to replenish her prenatal vitamins, worrying about André, eager to see him soon.

The handsome face commanding the cover of one of the tabloids changed her mind.

She picked it up, stared at the image, her blood chilling.

The photographers had captured André at various clubs and functions on the Riviera. Pictured him with a gorgeous woman on his arm. The headlines were disgustingly similar. Which beauty would win the billionaire's heart?

The fact he'd replaced Kira confirmed he'd never really cared about her at all. He'd fallen into the jet-setting lifestyle he'd supposedly despised. That told her she'd really never known him at all.

No wonder he wasn't eating or sleeping. He didn't have time!

She threw the tabloid down and marched from the store.

André Gauthier had cut her out of his life with surgical precision. It was past time she did the same. Time would heal this awful ache that stayed with her day and night, robbing her of sleep, of peace of mind. But she knew that the hole he left in her heart would never be mended, even after she did what she must do. Why did love have to hurt so much?

André stared pensively out the window of his private jet, anxious to set down, annoyed he was arriving in Las Vegas a week later than he'd intended. Exhaustion tormented every fiber of his being, having spent the most miserable month of his life throwing himself into work at his Riviera hotel—work he'd neglected when he'd decided to abduct Kira and take her to Petit St. Marc.

Kira. His heart gave a painful kick. He missed her more than he'd thought possible. Regret, fear and stubborn pride had kept him from calling her as he'd longed to do.

All his life he'd secretly feared he'd fall victim to a consuming passion like his parents had. To the eyes of a young boy,

his parents' heated fights and explosive ardor had been something to avoid.

He hadn't realized a man could love that deeply, that intently.
That a woman could become so much a part of him that losing
her was more painful and traumatic than losing an arm or leg,
that she pulsed through his blood and gave him life. That she
filled his heart and gave him hope.

He'd believed by walking away from her that he'd done the
right thing, for she was Edouard Bellamy's daughter. To admit
he had lost his heart to her would mean his enemy had won.

But he'd been wrong.

When he'd walked away from Kira he'd lost the best thing
that had ever happened to him. He'd been a fool to believe her
mother's claim that Edouard was Kira's father, to let that prob-
ability poison him.

The woman had *sold* her daughter to Bellamy. Why? *Was*
Bellamy her father? Or the wealthiest former lover that her
mother had been able to con?

André had to know the truth, which was why he'd charged
his detective with digging deeper into her past. But the answers
he sought eluded him still.

What did it matter anyway? If Bellamy was her father, then
he would find a way to deal with it. He could not alter the fact
any more than he could rearrange the sun and the moon—any
more than he could change the past.

The past was just that—the past.

His future was with Kira.

She was his woman. The mother of his child. He'd do
anything to gain her favor and forgiveness. To win her heart.

She'd resist him out of hurt pride at the very least. But he'd
captured her heart before. He would do it again. Only this time
he'd never let her go.

The sun was just starting to graze the expanse of glass and
steel stretching down the Las Vegas strip when André walked

into the Chateau Mystique. Unlike before, he marched straight to the front desk and announced that he must speak with Kira immediately.

"Your name, sir?" the clerk asked, the image of poised efficiency that he himself demanded in all his own hotels and resorts.

"Gauthier. André Gauthier."

The clerk's eyes widened a fraction, to hint that she recognized his name. "One moment, please," she said, and hurried off into the manager's office, situated at the end of the long cherrywood counter topped with rich pink granite.

Before André could stew about the wait, the door to the office opened and the clerk motioned him in. "This way, sir."

"Thank you."

André's gut tightened, his heart thudding far too fast as he strode to the door. He knew what he must say, what he wanted to tell Kira. But he wasn't poetic, and he had certainly lost his patience.

He'd simply blurt it out, then take her in his arms and kiss her. Everything else would fall into place then.

She'd forgive him for being a high-handed ass. Maybe not today, but soon.

She'd agree that they would get married immediately, for he couldn't bear to wait any longer.

She'd take him in her arms and ease this terrible ache that had filled him since he'd left her in the hospital, for she was the most loving, most genuinely good woman he'd ever met in his life.

André closed the door to afford him and Kira privacy.

Only Kira wasn't in the room. A young, dignified man rose from behind the desk to greet him, his smile polite yet wary.

"How may I help you, Monsieur Gauthier?" the man asked.

André didn't mince words—didn't have the time or the patience to jump through hoops. "I must speak with Kira Montgomery immediately."

The young man let out a nervous laugh. "I'm sorry, sir, but Miss Montgomery isn't here."

André inhaled deeply and blew it out in frustration. Fine. He would wait.

"When will she return?"

"I don't know," the manager said. "She left a week ago and told me not to expect her back anytime soon."

He hadn't anticipated that. The Chateau meant the world to Kira. She wouldn't leave it indefinitely unless something pressing had come up.

Fear lanced through him. *Mon Dieu*, the baby!

"Is she all right? Where did she go?" André asked.

The manager stiffened, his smile replaced by a professional mask. "I can't divulge that."

André gritted his teeth. Loyalty could be an annoying quality in employees. "Then tell me how I can contact her."

The manager gave a wry laugh. "Sir, I was left with strict orders that Miss Montgomery was not to be disturbed, unless there is a pressing problem at the Chateau that I can't handle."

André slammed both palms on the table and leaned forward, crowding the young manager's space, ready to beat the truth out of the cheeky man if he must. "I am André Gauthier, and I demand to speak with Miss Montgomery. Now, where the *hell* is she?"

"She mentioned being homesick," the manager said. "Before you ask, she didn't divulge where her home happened to be."

That couldn't be. The Chateau was her home. "You are sure?"

"Yes, sir."

He stormed from the office, so angry at himself he could have bellowed his rage. She shouldn't be traveling in her condition.

And just where *was* home? England? The boarding school where she'd spent the bulk of her life?

The possibilities were endless. The fear that he could lose her seeped into his bones, rattling his confidence, shaking his world.

His hand shook as he called his investigator. "I need to know where Kira Montgomery has gone on holiday."

"I'll get right on it," his private detective said. "As for the paternity issue—Bellamy was cremated. Blood type can reveal if it was possible for him to have been her father, but it won't prove conclusively if he actually is."

"Forget it, then. Just find Kira."

He stormed from the Chateau and arranged to return to Petit St. Marc. He'd wait there, worry, throw himself into work to keep from losing his mind.

But, no matter how long it took, he'd not give up finding her and making her his.

André stormed into his house, barely acknowledging Otillie waiting at the door, her face wreathed in an effusive smile.

"Bonsoir, Monsieur Gauthier," she said. *"Comment allez-vous?"*

"Exhausted," he said. As well as angry, and worried sick, and in no mood for pleasantries.

He strode to the stairs just before that subtle floral scent snared him, that silken string of remembrance bringing him up short. Just like he'd been tormented in his dreams. Only this was real. Kira!

He whirled, scanning his house, alert, hoping to hell that he hadn't finally gone mad and imagined her. "Where is she?"

Otillie laughed. His opinionated Carib housekeeper, who'd taken a dislike to Kira when she'd barged into his house months ago, who'd been furious with him for going after her and bringing her here, was laughing with great pleasure.

"Mademoiselle is in the salon," she said at last.

Heart beating savagely against his ribs, André crossed the hall in six long strides. He stopped in the doorway and leaned against the jamb, simply because he wasn't sure his legs would carry him the rest of the way.

For a long moment he drank in the sight of Kira curled on his sofa, looking radiant and inviting in his home. Their home.

Mon Dieu, what a fool he'd been. She'd told her staff she

was going home. She considered Petit St. Marc home. Thought his house was hers. That had to be a good sign.

She was here with him at last—had returned to him of her own accord. All would be well.

But, no, she was frowning at him now, looking wary. Unapproachable.

His blood pounded with the need to touch her, kiss her, love her. At this moment he felt every inch the pirate, rugged and ruthless, uncouth and unashamed of grabbing the spoils of war. For this fabulous English rose was his booty.

He'd wanted her the first time she barged into his office. He'd taken her, believing she was involved in the cutthroat war he'd waged with Bellamy. He'd continued to take her even when doubts had encroached.

She'd deserved so much more than the cold life meted out to her by Bellamy. She certainly hadn't deserved André's hostility, his constant doubts over her innocence, his refusal to give her anything but physical love.

Oui, he was unworthy of her. That was why he'd walked away from her that day in the hospital.

But he couldn't let go of her. He, who'd vowed never to let a woman embed herself in his heart and soul, caught himself thinking about her during his days, dreaming about her during the long, lonely nights.

He loved her. The admission came hard for a man who had vowed never to fall victim to that crippling emotion. But refusing to admit it crippled him more, for he was haunted by her smile, her touch, her love.

No, he couldn't let her go. Not now. Not ever.

He pushed away from the doorway and strode to her, stopping when he reached her side. His fingers curled into fists, trembling, for he knew if he touched her he'd tumble her back on the sofa and caress her everywhere. Make love to her, here, now, without a modicum of finesse.

"Marry me," he said.

Her eyes bugged and her inviting lips parted. "What?"

A gruff sound of impatience rumbled in his throat. "You look beautiful. You are pregnant with my child, *mon amour*. Marry me."

She flushed, her body stiffening, putting up a wall he hated, one that would geld him should he attempt jumping it. But he would jump it.

"I was pregnant a month ago, when you rushed me to the hospital, yet you didn't offer marriage then," she said.

Touché—a direct hit. Damn, but he was doing this badly. "I was an ass."

"And now you're not?"

He drove his fingers through his hair, frustrated, trembling like a schoolboy, tasting fear and despising it. For if he said the wrong thing she'd never marry him.

Mon Dieu, was this the tangled emotion that had gripped his father? That had made him act the fool with his mother?

"I am the father of your child," he said. "The man you love."

"True." She stared at him a long, uncomfortable moment. "But you hate all Bellamys. You've spent considerable time and money to destroy Edouard's dynasty and ruin Peter. Need I remind you that I am Edouard Bellamy's daughter?"

"I hate Bellamy, not you. Never you, *mon amour*."

She squirmed, seeming to grow more nervous by the second. "You say that now, but what about a month from now? A year?"

"I've treated you badly. *Us* badly." He knelt at her side and laid a hand over her stomach, trembling as heat shot from her into him, feeling their bond clear to his soul. "What must I do to convince you that I want you as my wife, as the mother of my child? That I wish to grow old with you?"

Her gaze softened, her lips trembling into a smile as she reached out and cupped his jaw in her hands, her touch seeping into his skin, his blood, his heart. "I want to believe you, but blood is telling, André. I have to be sure you will not resent me because I am a Bellamy, because our baby has the same blood."

"Our child is Gauthier," he said, leaning forward to kiss her once, twice. How had he lived without kissing her the past month?

"And part Bellamy," she said, pulling back.

He sighed, hating the caution still banked in her expressive eyes, hating that he was responsible for putting it there, dreading how she'd accept his last confession. "Maybe yes, maybe no. I had my investigator attempt to prove you are Bellamy's daughter, but without Edouard's DNA it's impossible to determine."

"We'll never know, then," she said. "There will always be that doubt."

"Only if you let uncertainty torment you." He cupped her face in his hands and stared into her eyes, his own shining with a warmth and affection that she'd only seen in her dreams. "*Ma chérie*, everything you know and believe about yourself is the same."

"I'm afraid to hope."

"So was I. Which is why I had to look in here for the answer." He thumped a fist on his heart. "I realized that I'd fallen in love with you even when I thought you were Edouard Bellamy's puppet, and I continued to long for you even when I was sure you were Peter's mistress. When I thought you'd conspired to ruin me I still loved you. It nearly drove me mad to admit that despite what I believed of you I wanted you as my lover, my wife."

"Oh, André, you love me?"

"Eternally. You are in my blood, my skin," he said. "My heart pounds for you. Marry me, *mon coeur*. Be mine forever."

"Yes," she said, wrapping her arms around his neck and kissing him back.

André pulled her against him, pouring his heart and soul into the kiss, his hands roaming her back, her slightly thicker waist, her small belly where their child thrived. "We will marry next week."

"Why the rush?"

"Need you ask?"

He caressed her belly, pleased by the mound there now. His throat felt thick, his heart was thudding too loud.

His woman. His child. He'd considered them his before, but the depth of what that meant hadn't hit him until he'd nearly lost her.

"I don't want a big wedding," she said. "Something quiet."

"*Oui*, intimate. We can marry here."

"I'd love that." She kissed his cheek and sighed, a contented sound that rumbled in him as well. "I love you."

"*Mon amour.*" He trailed kisses up her neck, addicted to the taste of her skin, her scent, her love. "*Mon coeur.*"

"I need to learn French," she said.

"We will start now. Repeat after me. *Je t'aime, avec tout mon coeur.*"

She did, saying each word slowly, carefully. "What did I just say to you?"

"I love you," he said, "with all my heart."

She smiled, blinking rapidly, her love for him shining in her eyes. "It's true."

He kissed her, a soft lingering kiss that dragged a sigh from her. "I love you, Kira Montgomery. That's all that matters. You are mine and I am yours and we have created our own family."

She smiled and felt her heart melt, felt a sense of home and harmony envelop her. For he was right. She'd found her family in his arms, her future in his heart.

As long as they had each other, nothing else mattered.

After five months of having a protective husband indulge her with his attention and his passion—until the latter had proved too great a risk—and after enduring a killing backache for the past few days, Kira made a speedy trip back to the hospital on Martinique.

As before, André insisted on holding her as the captain

drove the *Sans Doute* at breakneck speed. This time she was able to see the love and worry in her husband's eyes, and her heart melted all over again.

This time, instead of nearly losing her baby, she gave birth to Antoine Louis Gauthier. The nearly nine-pound boy had his father's piercing dark eyes and beautifully sculpted mouth, but he had inherited her broader nose and auburn hair.

Her heart overflowed with love as she trailed a finger along her son's plump cheek, hardly able to believe that their small family circle had been completed.

Family. She could scarce believe her new life was real.

She had prayed she'd one day have a family all her life, but she'd never dreamed that she'd have a husband who openly adored her. That she'd deliver a healthy child to complete that circle of love.

Family. Never again would she live on the fringe of her relatives, the unwanted child nobody spoke of.

For her husband wanted her. And now she and André had a son. She was certain Antoine would be spoiled rotten by his adoring parents.

He'd never doubt he was loved. Wanted. Cherished.

André sat on the bed, his eyes glittering with adoration. "My son has a healthy appetite," he said, as she nursed Antoine for the first time.

"He's his father's son."

"*Oui*, he is."

A proud smile curved André's sensual mouth. Her husband no longer guarded his emotions around her, a fact that had allowed them to draw closer.

"He's beautiful," André said. "Thank you, *mon coeur*."

She smiled, thankful, and so happy that she couldn't stop tears of joy from spilling from her eyes. This was contentment. This was love.

He shifted closer to her and their son. "It has been too long since I was part of a family."

"Having a family is a whole new world to me, but then so is marriage and being a wife and a mother. It takes getting used to."

"Regrets?" he asked.

"None." She smiled, understanding this complex man who guarded his heart so well, loving him, wanting him. "It's been too long since you kissed me."

"Then I must remedy that, *mon coeur*," he said, his eyes glistening with love as his head dipped to hers.

HARLEQUIN *Presents*

TWO CROWNS, TWO ISLANDS, ONE LEGACY

*A royal family torn apart by pride and lust for power,
reunited by purity and passion*

Pick up the next adventure in this passionate series!

Eight volumes to collect and treasure!

HARLEQUIN *Presents*

REQUEST YOUR FREE BOOKS!

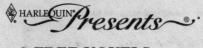

2 FREE NOVELS
PLUS 2
FREE GIFTS!

YES! Please send me 2 FREE Harlequin Presents® novels and my 2 FREE gifts (gifts are worth about $10). After receiving them, if I don't wish to receive any more books, I can return the shipping statement marked "cancel". If I don't cancel, I will receive 6 brand-new novels every month and be billed just $4.05 per book in the U.S. or $4.74 per book in Canada. That's a savings of close to 15% off the cover price! It's quite a bargain! Shipping and handling is just 50¢ per book*. I understand that accepting the 2 free books and gifts places me under no obligation to buy anything. I can always return a shipment and cancel at any time. Even if I never buy another book, the two free books and gifts are mine to keep forever.   106 HDN EYRQ 306 HDN EYR2

Name	(PLEASE PRINT)	
Address		Apt. #
City	State/Prov.	Zip/Postal Code

Signature (if under 18, a parent or guardian must sign)

Mail to the **Harlequin Reader Service:**
IN U.S.A.: P.O. Box 1867, Buffalo, NY 14240-1867
IN CANADA: P.O. Box 609, Fort Erie, Ontario L2A 5X3

Not valid to current subscribers of Harlequin Presents books.

Are you a current subscriber of Harlequin Presents books and want to receive the larger-print edition? Call 1-800-873-8635 today!

* Terms and prices subject to change without notice. Prices do not include applicable taxes. Sales tax applicable in N.Y. Canadian residents will be charged applicable provincial taxes and GST. Offer not valid in Quebec. This offer is limited to one order per household. All orders subject to approval. Credit or debit balances in a customer's account(s) may be offset by any other outstanding balance owed by or to the customer. Please allow 4 to 6 weeks for delivery. Offer available while quantities last.

HP09R

ROYAL AND RUTHLESS

Royally bedded, regally wedded!

A Mediterranean majesty, a Greek prince, a desert king and a fierce nobleman—with any of these men around, a royal bedding is imminent!

And when they're done in the bedroom, the next thing to arrange is a very regal wedding!

Look for all of these fabulous stories available in August 2009!

Innocent Mistress, Royal Wife #65
by ROBYN DONALD

The Ruthless Greek's Virgin Princess #66
by TRISH MOREY

The Desert King's Bejewelled Bride #67
by SABRINA PHILIPS

Veretti's Dark Vengeance #68
by LUCY GORDON

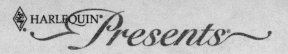

Coming Next Month

#2843 THE PLAYBOY SHEIKH'S VIRGIN STABLE-GIRL
Sharon Kendrick
The Royal House of Karedes

#2844 RUTHLESS BILLIONAIRE, FORBIDDEN BABY Emma Darcy

#2845 THE MARCOLINI BLACKMAIL MARRIAGE Melanie Milburne

#2846 BLACKMAILED INTO THE GREEK TYCOON'S BED
Carol Marinelli
International Billionaires

#2847 BOUGHT: FOR HIS CONVENIENCE OR PLEASURE?
Maggie Cox

#2848 SPANISH MAGNATE, RED-HOT REVENGE Lynn Raye Harris

#2849 PLAYBOY BOSS, PREGNANCY OF PASSION Kate Hardy
To Tame a Playboy

#2850 NAUGHTY NIGHTS IN THE MILLIONAIRE'S MANSION
Robyn Grady
Nights of Passion

Plus, look out for the fabulous new collection
Royal and Ruthless from Harlequin® Presents® EXTRA:

#65 INNOCENT MISSTRESS, ROYAL WIFE
Robyn Donald

#66 THE RUTHLESS GREEK'S VIRGIN PRINCESS
Trish Morey

#67 THE DESERT KING'S BEJEWELLED BRIDE
Sabrina Philips

#68 VERETTI'S DARK VENGEANCE
Lucy Gordon